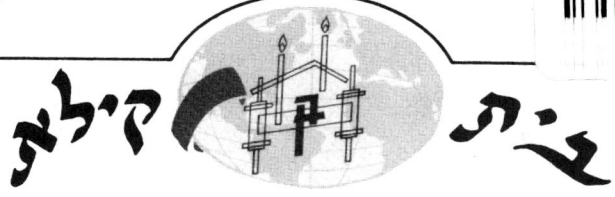

BAIS KAILA
TORAH PREPARATORY
HIGH SCHOOL FOR GIRLS

*proudly presents
this fascinating volume
to its many friends
and supporters*

Our New Lakewood Campus

Located in the world famous Torah community of Lakewood, New Jersey, Bais Kaila High School provides the ultimate in Torah-oriented education for girls. Bais Kaila girls are motivated and encouraged to reach their full potential intellectually and spiritually, with particular emphasis on good *midos* and solid ethical and moral values.

To receive additional copies of this book or to have a friend included in our future mailings please write to:

BAIS KAILA HIGH SCHOOL
Spruce and Vine Streets, P.O.B. 952, Lakewood, New Jersey 08701

More information about the background and educational programs of Bais Kaila High School appears at the back of the book.

On a Golden Chain

a novel by
Ruth Benjamin

C·I·S
P·U·B·L·I·S·H·E·R·S
New York · London · Jerusalem

Copyright © 1991

All rights reserved.
This book, or any part thereof,
may not be reproduced in any
form whatsoever without the express
written permission of the copyright holder.

Published and distributed
in the U.S., Canada and overseas by
C.I.S. Publishers and Distributors
180 Park Avenue, Lakewood, New Jersey 08701
(908) 905-3000 Fax: (908) 367-6666

Distributed in Israel by
C.I.S. International (Israel)
Rechov Mishkalov 18
Har Nof, Jerusalem
Tel: 02-538-935

Distributed in the U.K. and Europe by
C.I.S. International (U.K.)
89 Craven Park Road
London N15 6AH, England
Tel: 01-809-3723

Book and cover design: Deenee Cohen
Typography: Chaya Bleier
Cover photography: Solaria Studios

ISBN 1-56062-080-3 hard cover
1-56062-081-1 soft cover

Library of Congress Catalog Card Number
91-73666

PRINTED IN THE UNITED STATES OF AMERICA

with thanks to:

Rabbi Yisroel Shusterman

Rabbi Nachum Meir Bernhard

Rabbi Levi Wineberg

Rabbi Moshe Doman

Ruth Bolnick

Yehudis Gralnik

Leah Saban

and Raizy Kaufman, of C.I.S. Publishers,
for her stimulating guidance and ready patience.
Her unfailing encouragement has been
deeply appreciated.

CHAPTER 1

"Oh, Nana, she's pretty. She's really, really pretty. I just love her!" Lucy stroked the doll's long golden curls, stared into its large, blue eyes framed by thick eyelashes and hugged it gently. "You knew just what to buy me for my birthday! I just love her!"

Steven stood by, a little uncertainly. He knew it wasn't his birthday and therefore there was no present due him, but he couldn't help but feel a little jealous of his sister's present. Even he, who would seldom give dolls a second glance, had to admit the doll was beautiful.

His grandmother came over to him. "Steven," she said. "I haven't forgotten about you. I know it isn't your birthday, but I got you a small something, nevertheless."

The old lady went to her cupboard and took

out a small, compact, very realistic steam train engine. It was black and shiny with green markings. It had sturdy silver wheels and a fully dressed engine driver.

"I bought batteries and it really goes," she said. "I already put them in. All you have to do is to switch it on. It doesn't need to run on tracks."

He put the train on the floor and switched it on. It emitted a sharp whistle and started to chug along the floor, blowing out tiny puffs of smoke.

Even Lucy's attention was caught, and she brought her doll with her to look at it.

"Wow," she said. "It really works! It really smokes!"

Steven was delighted with his new toy. He watched it make its own circles and noted the way it would avoid any obstacles placed in its way. Suddenly, however, he walked over to it and switched it off. He sat down next to it, an anxious look on his face.

"What's the matter, Steven?" his grandmother asked. "Why do you look so worried?"

Steven stared at her for a few seconds, not knowing if he should speak. Finally, he said, "Nana, what will Mummy say?"

"She won't mind," she said, a puzzled look in her eyes. "She knows that when I give one of you a birthday present I always give a small present to the other one."

"Yes, but . . ." Steven seemed embarrassed and his grandmother became more puzzled. "Yes, but a train. What will Mummy say about a train?"

His grandmother was suddenly serious. "What do you mean, Stevie?" she asked, her voice becoming guarded. "Why should she mind a train?"

Steven looked unhappy. "Mummy has dreams," he said. "She dreams about trains."

"Did she tell you she dreams about trains?" she asked.

"No," he said. "No, she never talks to me about that, but I heard her talking to Daddy. It upsets her very much. She dreams about trains like other people dream about monsters. I suppose trains can be frightening."

He seemed to lose his anxiety and once more switched on the train, again becoming excited about its tiny puffs of smoke. He looked at it fondly.

"Mummy won't be scared of you, little train, I am sure she won't," he said. "You are such a smart, good little train. But you wouldn't hurt anyone, would you? I think Mummy will love you."

They heard a car outside the cottage, and the children ran out to meet their parents who had dropped them off for a short time while they had gone to buy some soda for Nana, which was always far too heavy for Nana to carry on her own. They had tried for years to dissuade her from doing any of her heavy shopping on foot, but she continued to disregard their pleas, reassuring them that she had walked to the shops and returned with parcels for almost sixty years, and why should she change now?

Richard and Dorothy Wilson admired the toys Dorothy's mother had bought for their children. The doll truly was beautiful, and the train?

"Magnificent," said Richard.

"It's incredible," said Dorothy. "It's almost real. Look, it puffs real smoke!"

Her mother watched her carefully. Was Dorothy really still anxious about trains, to the point of becoming upset about a toy train? She recalled that she herself had had to comfort her as a child on countless occasions.

But Dorothy did not seem affected by the train, and the family was soon drinking tea from Nana's gold rimmed china teacups with large English roses on them.

ON A GOLDEN CHAIN

Nana had made a special cake for Lucy's birthday. She had iced it herself, and had obviously taken several hours to do so. It was a delicate shade of pink, with darker pink roses and emerald green leaves. In the center was a fairy with a billowing skirt, also made of icing.

"Nana, I must keep this cake," said Lucy. "I can't let anything ever, ever happen to it."

Her grandmother laughed, delighted with Lucy's reaction. She had worked hard, but she had enjoyed it.

"I have always loved decorating cakes for my little girls," she said.

Dorothy cast her mind back to the time when she, too, had been a little girl. Each birthday had seen a different cake. There was a clown, a cat, a princess, a castle, a village and many other things. In fact, most of those had been photographed and were placed proudly in a family album.

She remembered the parties she had had, always with only a few children, but always expertly catered by her mother, always something special, to be remembered. Her father would help with the games to entertain the children, setting up fairly complicated equipment.

She felt a stab of pain as she thought of him. Had ten years already passed since he had died? Why had that sense of emptiness still not left her?

Her mother, she could see, still mourned every day for him. She had never been the same since he had died.

Both her parents had been older than any of her friends' parents. In fact, they had been more in the age group of many of their grandparents. She was an only child, obviously born when they were fairly advanced in years, and she had loved them dearly.

She pictured her father as he had been in earlier years, before he had become so ill. He had always been a person who kept to himself. He would arrive home from work and then spend many hours in the workshop at the back of the house. His hobby had been carpentry, but he had never made anything he was prepared to sell. His house was full of beautifully carved pieces, priceless, she was sure.

Both he and her mother had been perfectionists. She remembered how she used to sit with her father for many hours in his workshop, chatting to him and doing odd jobs for him.

She remembered, too, the distinctive way in which he would sometimes speak, especially when he was excited or tired. It was almost as if he had a foreign accent. And yet, as far as she knew, her parents had never been out of England.

She had always been very close to her parents, regarding them as her best friends. She was aware that she had always been the center of their lives. Anyone with less sensitivity and intelligence might, in that position, have become thoroughly spoiled and disagreeable. They had given her everything and had done everything they could for her. She had gone to the best schools, had gone to college and had been given a car as soon as she had graduated. Anything she had expressed a wish for, she was given, if not immediately, at her very next birthday.

Her mother tended to spoil Dorothy's children, too, in this way. Nothing was too good or too expensive for them.

She was interrupted from her reverie by Lucy coming over to her with her doll.

"What shall I call her, Mummy? What do you think her name should be?"

"My favorite doll was called Esther," Dorothy said slowly. "She was lovely. In fact, she looked a little bit like this doll."

"Come, Esther," said Lucy, smoothing out the doll's dress. "Come and see Steven's train."

CHAPTER

2

"We must be leaving now, Mum," Dorothy said. "It's getting late and I must give the kids supper and get them into bed, though I can't imagine what they'll eat after all your biscuits and sausage rolls and cakes. In fact, I don't think Richard or I feel like eating either. Maybe we'll just have some soup and bread. That will be more than enough."

Dorothy collected her children's sweaters, sweets and other possessions and acquisitions and prepared to leave. Her mother followed them to the door.

"I wonder if you would drop by and fetch me for the women's meeting in church tomorrow morning," she said. "Until now, I have always walked, but the weather has been quite hot and I find I become tired if I walk too far."

Dorothy was anxious. That was not like her mother. The church was not far, and Nana had always insisted that she needed the walk for exercise. Wasn't she feeling well?

"Are you all right, Mum?" she asked, trying to keep any hint of worry out of her voice.

"Of course I am, Dorothy. I am a hundred percent well. I'm just a little tired, that's all." She looked somewhat irritated.

"Shouldn't you see a doctor?" Dorothy continued.

"A doctor!" said her mother. "Doctors make you worse. They pronounce all kinds of illnesses on you, and then that's what you are and what you've got. I should never have taken your father to a doctor. Maybe he would have been alive today! Never mind. If it causes so much trouble I will walk."

"No," said Richard. "Of course Dorothy will take you to the meeting, and she'll fetch you afterwards. You must not walk!"

"I don't want you to consider me an invalid," the old lady said. "I can look after myself."

Her face suddenly turned a chalky white, and she started to sway. She held on to Dorothy's arms for a few seconds.

"There is something happening with you, Mum," she said. "There is something the matter."

"It's nothing. It's just one of my little spells," said her mother. "Everyone gets them at my age. I just need a little water and I will be fine."

They helped her back to the couch and sat her down. The children were subdued. Dorothy brought her mother a glass of water.

"Please let me call the doctor, Mum," she said. "You've got to let me call him. I can't bear the thought of anything happening to you. Please be all right!"

"Don't worry, Dorothy," said her mother.

ON A GOLDEN CHAIN

Richard had put a footrest beneath her feet and had gone to fetch a blanket. Nana was already looking better. Her color had returned and she was beginning to look more cheerful. She begged them to go home, but they refused. For the next twenty minutes she did not protest, but finally she said, "You should all go home. Don't worry about me. I'll be fine. This has happened to me before, and after a good sleep I have been just fine. My grandchildren are looking really sleepy. They need to eat and go to bed."

Dorothy looked at them. Lucy was cradling her doll in her arms, a sleepy expression on her face, while Steven was patting his train quite mechanically. They *were* tired, and so, probably, was Nana. She had worked very hard on the party. She must have been standing for hours icing the cake. She had a right to be tired. Everyone had a right to be tired.

They stayed a few more minutes until she was truly back to herself and then left.

An hour and a half later, Richard and Dorothy were sitting in their living room. They had snacked, put the children to bed and phoned to make sure Nana was all right, and for the first time that day, they really relaxed.

"I'm playing football this Saturday," said Richard. "Our team is playing Bridgley. It should be a knockout win for us. I hope you are bringing the kids to watch us."

"Of course I will," said Dorothy. "They love to come. They are very proud of their Dad."

Richard smiled and turned on the television to a sports program. Dorothy knew that for the next hour at least there would be no way she could speak to him. She sat, vaguely watching the game in front of her, busy with her thoughts.

She was worried about her mother, and again this brought back painful memories about her father's illness and death. She tried to force her mind away from these thoughts.

She had been devastated when her father had died. She and her mother had clung to one another for several months after that until her mother had made it clear that her daughter had her own life to lead, and that she should meet someone and get married.

She had not been so keen on doing this. The local boys somehow didn't interest her, and though she was pleasant enough to them she would never have dreamed of becoming seriously involved with them. Whenever anyone made a suggestion, she simply laughed and changed the subject.

This was until she met Richard, tall, sandy-haired, with eyes that seemed to be able to change to almost any color from greenish-blue to brown. In his college years, he had been captain of several sports teams.

Life, for her, had begun to change. Almost from the first time she met him, she knew that this was the man she wanted to marry. He obviously had the same idea, and it was not long before they were engaged. Sometime during their courtship, Richard had mentioned with some embarrassment that his mother had once been Jewish, but it had meant nothing. She had become a Presbyterian when she had married his father. He, of course, though he had some Jewish blood, did not regard this of any importance, and so, neither did she. Who would know, anyway? He had been very careful that no one should find out.

Strangely enough, however, over the years, even after his mother's and then his father's death, thoughts of Richard's Jewish connection had often come back to her. She often wondered vaguely why this was so. It wasn't bad to be Jewish. In fact, she didn't really know much about Jews, or why Richard should be embarrassed about having some Jewish blood.

She went to the kitchen, poured two cups of coffee, and

set one down before her husband who was engrossed with the television show.

Two children had been born to them, a boy and a girl. They were religious and went to church every Sunday. The children were enrolled at the local school. Richard had a good job. They had an above average house, lived in a sought-after area, had many friends. Everything was good. They were a "model" family.

The sports program was coming to an end. Richard was emerging from his trance. He smiled apologetically. "Sorry," he said. "I just had to see that. I couldn't concentrate on anything until I saw what would happen with that other team."

He tried to sip the coffee and looked at Dorothy. "Why is my coffee cold?" was written all over his face.

She laughed. "I'll make you another cup," she said. "It's only that you were in another world. It was hot, very hot, when I put it down in front of you."

"I believe you," he said. "And when you do make me another cup, please make it cocoa. Coffee sometimes keeps me awake and it's getting quite late."

When she came back, he was sitting on the carpet watching Steven's train engine going round and round, producing its puffs of smoke.

"It seems you like the train as much as your son does," she said. "You must remember to put it back in his room, otherwise he will think it has been hijacked."

"Don't worry, I will," he said. "I even made sure I had some extra batteries in my drawer. He would have wondered why these batteries ran out."

She watched her husband playing with the toy train, putting obstacles in its way and watching the train avoid them. As she watched, however, she found her level of tension increasing. She suddenly couldn't bear to watch that train.

"Please put it back in Steven's room," she said, a little sharply.

"I won't hurt it," said Richard. "I have other batteries if these run low. He won't notice I've been playing with it."

Dorothy continued to watch the train, and she began to feel sick as she watched it. "Please, Richard, please stop it. Otherwise I am going to bed."

He began to get irritated. "I'm not going to hurt it. It will be fine. If I break it I will buy him a new one. Why are you so worried about it?"

"Richard, Richard, it's upsetting me," she said. "I am frightened."

"Are you crazy?" he began, and then he realized what she was saying. "Your dreams," he said. "Trains. Is that it?"

"Yes," she said. "I'm sorry, Richard."

"Don't worry, Dot," he said, picking up the train. "I'll put this back. There's a good story coming up on television soon, and we'll watch it."

He good-naturedly took the train to Steven's room, came back and took a sip of his cocoa. The expression on his face said all over again, "Why is this cocoa cold?"

CHAPTER

3

There is a loud, sickening crash . . . blackness . . . a sound of tearing metal . . . incredible heat . . . the sound of dripping water . . . people screaming . . . flames . . . children crying . . . many people running . . . crawling . . . pushing . . . terror on their faces . . . railway carriages, twisted out of all proportion . . . people being carried out, crying, bleeding . . . some of them . . . so still . . . people lying side by side alongside the tracks . . . children . . .

She looks into a child's face . . . it is her face . . . except that it is covered in blood . . . she screams . . . . she is running through dark woods . . . tall trees . . . and she is screaming and screaming.

"Dorothy, Dorothy, wake up. Wake up! You are having that nightmare again. Wake up!"

As she heard Richard's voice, Dorothy felt herself being drawn slowly, almost reluctantly into the present. She was in a warm, comfortable bed. There was no train, no station, no screaming, no image of herself covered in blood. She was at home with her husband and her two children. She gave a sigh of relief. Why did that dream come so often to haunt her? Why *that* dream? She had heard of people having nightmares of falling, of monsters, or of getting lost, but why a train? And why so very, very real?

She looked at her clock and found it was five-thirty a.m. Too early to get up, but too late to go back to sleep. She looked towards Richard who was sleeping peacefully as if he had not woken her. She wished she had the ability to do that, to just wake up and go back to sleep as if nothing had happened. But it took her a long time to go to sleep if she was disturbed in any way. It just wasn't worth trying.

She got out of bed and went to the kitchen, stopping on the way to look into the mirror and to put some order to her short, dark curls. She looked closely at her blue eyes. She always had dark rings under them after the dream. Why did it bother her so much? She switched on the kettle to make some coffee.

She began to make the children's school lunches, taking her time to mash an egg salad and chop up vegetables to go with it. She added a pastry to each lunch box and then added a few chocolates. Very shortly the lunches were packed and the boxes put neatly on top of their briefcases.

Should she start with breakfast? No, it was still too early. The eggs would become congealed, and the toast would be cold. She sat at the table, sipping her coffee and thinking once more about her dream. It was always so realistic. So very, very realistic, almost as if she had been there.

But she hadn't been there. Her life had been so sheltered and uneventful. But why, then, the nightmares? Why was the vision of the train crash sent to haunt her? There was the vision of herself looking into her own face and her own body lying beside the railway track. Why the vision of herself running through the woods, terrified?

Strange. She must have read about it somewhere. Somewhere where it had made an impression on her. Perhaps she had seen it on television or in a movie. These things did happen in films.

This time, the toy train must have set it off. But the toy train had only come yesterday, and she had been having these dreams ever since she could remember. For nights and nights as a child she had lain in her parents arms, too afraid to go to sleep in case the dream came again.

She wasn't usually afraid of things. Only trains would provoke the most terrifying of feelings, feelings that her whole world would suddenly blow apart and change beyond recognition.

She wished that Richard were awake to talk to her. This hour of the morning could be so lonely. People were either asleep or too busy preparing themselves for early work to spend any time chatting. This would be considered an unearthly hour to phone anyone, even her best friends.

Did she have best friends? Her best friends at school, though she was still in contact with them, had become all but acquaintances. They met one another's husbands and children and spent afternoons and evenings with them, but there could no longer be any of the long discussions they had shared together at school. At school, they had swapped concepts and philosophies of life. Today they swapped recipes and anecdotes of their children. Pleasant interaction it was, but best, trusted friends? Somehow they were no longer that. Her best friends today were her husband and her children. Perhaps that is how it should be. In fact, she was sure that's how it should be. She poured herself another cup of coffee. It would be at least an hour before she could speak to anyone who might be awake.

Of course, there was her mother. She could, she knew, phone her at any time of the day or night, and her mother would be really pleased to speak to her.

She walked over to the phone and then hesitated. Mum had been very tired the day before. She had worked really hard for Lucy's party. Everything had been done to perfection the way it always was.

A chill suddenly went through Dorothy. Was her mother really ill? What if something would happen to her? She had always seemed so strong, so well, so capable, even when her heart was breaking from her husband's death. She had a strength that seemed to be almost indestructible, but yesterday she had not been herself.

It had been years since she had really seen a doctor. For Dorothy doctors had been fine and necessary, but for herself, she had evaded them almost completely.

Dorothy decided then that she would put her foot down and insist. Her mother had to see a doctor. She would make an appointment as soon as the doctor's office opened.

CHAPTER 4

The phone rang loudly, jolting Dorothy out of her thoughts. That was unusual. Who would phone at this hour of the morning? Perhaps it was a wrong number.

She shook a little as she lifted the receiver. "Hello," she said. "Hello, hello?"

There seemed to be no one at the other end, but then she heard her mother's voice, fainter than usual. "Dorothy, dear, I'm sorry to call so early. Perhaps you could come over. I'm not feeling too well."

Dorothy's heart started to pound. "Of course, Mum. I'm coming right away," she said and put down the receiver. She rushed into the bedroom.

"Richard," she said. "Something is wrong with Mum. I have to take the car and go see her right away."

ON A GOLDEN CHAIN

Within minutes, she was again driving along the road towards the home in which she had grown up, the beautiful cottage set in the garden tended lovingly, first by her father and then her mother. It was full of miniature roses and beds of violets. All the time, she was throwing recriminations at herself. Why hadn't they stayed with Mum overnight? They had known she was not well.

She rang the door bell but there was no answer. Frantically, she put her key in the lock. Thank goodness, she had brought it with her.

The cottage was very still. She found her mother collapsed in a chair next to the telephone, her skin a strange, purplish color.

Dorothy picked up the telephone and with trembling hands, dialed the number of the doctor and was soon speaking to him. He would be over right away.

Her mother was moaning, her eyes shut. Her color seemed to be getting worse, and her skin had taken on a grayish tinge. Dorothy stroked her hair, and quite suddenly her mother seemed to recover a little.

"Dorothy," she said, trying to smile through the pain. "I am glad you came. I have something to tell you . . . before I go . . . before I die . . . ."

"Mum, you are not going to die," said Dorothy, a coldness grasping at her heart. "I called the doctor."

"I was never one for doctors," her mother said. "He will be too late." Dorothy was about to protest, but her mother seemed to want to tell her something.

"Dorothy," she said, and her voice seemed to be getting weaker. "Dorothy, our Dorothy. We have loved you more than anything in the world. But we are not your parents, Dorothy. We don't know who your parents are. We found you, running through the forest, terrified, not knowing who you were. You were only four or five years old at the time.

"We took you in, just for a few days, until someone would look for you. But no one did, and after some weeks we realized we could not part with you. Your parents must have been killed in the train crash. Nearly everyone was killed.

"Dorothy, for years and years I have wondered if we had a right to do what we did. Your father kept telling me it was right and good, and he believed it sincerely. But since he has gone, I have had doubts. I have had visions of your family looking for you, accusing faces that come to me in my dreams. I know now that I could not keep this from you.

"We had tried and tried to have children, but we never did. And then you came. We called you Dorothy. You were a gift from Heaven, and we loved you. We loved you so much, and you loved us.

"We were afraid," her mother continued. "We were afraid that one day someone, a cousin, an uncle, would come and claim you, that someone who didn't love you as we loved you would recognize you and take you away. So we moved here, to a far, far distant place where no one would know you and no one knew us, and we were just mother, father and daughter. We have been happy here."

Dorothy wanted to ask more questions but her mother continued, her voice reduced to a gasp. "There is no more time now. There is a gold chain in my jewelry chest on top of my dresser, a chain which you were wearing when we found you. On it is a star of David, a Jewish star of David, a small Jewish star . . . a star on a golden chain."

A look of pain and shock passed over her face and she suddenly relaxed and was very, very still.

"Mum, Mum," cried Dorothy. But it was no use. Her mother was dead.

The doorbell rang. It was Doctor Simons. He came

straight over to her mother and examined her for a few minutes.

"She's gone," he said briefly. "I am sorry. Shall I contact your husband for you?"

Dorothy felt numb as she heard this. Her mother—gone? Impossible! Nana was indestructible! She couldn't be gone! She wanted to tell the doctor that he had made a terrible mistake, that he hadn't examined her as well as he could have, that he had missed something, a heartbeat, anything! She wanted to rant and rave and shout at him for slicing her life in half with a few words. Perhaps her mother would be all right the next day. Surely she was dreaming! She must be dreaming!

This was her mother!

A thought suddenly struck Dorothy. This wasn't her mother. She had told her before she died that she wasn't her real mother. If she wasn't her mother, then who was her mother? She suddenly felt faint.

"Sit down," the doctor said. "You have had a terrible shock. I will speak to your husband and, of course, your minister. He needs to attend to all the arrangements. Please give me his name."

"Yes, yes," she said. "It's Rev. Purdy. He is our . . . he is my mother's minister."

CHAPTER 5

Rev. Ian Purdy looked first at Dorothy and then at Richard. It was several days after the funeral, and it was the first time they had had time to talk to him about Dorothy's mother's final words to her daughter.

Dorothy had found the small star of David in the jewelry chest on top of the dresser. She had looked through the chest, hoping there would be something else which would point to her past, but there was only the key and number to a bank safe deposit box, amidst the bracelets, necklaces and odd bits of jewelry.

As the whole matter involved many religious questions, they decided to speak to the minister. It seemed that Dorothy was probably Jewish.

"I wouldn't worry about it," the minister was saying. "After all, no one would really suspect.

ON A GOLDEN CHAIN

You look a perfectly respectable Christian family—mother, father, two children—staunch churchgoers. You don't *look* Jewish or anything. At least, not markedly so. You don't have to worry about people finding out. I am a minister of religion, and I keep things confidential."

"But," said Dorothy, "I would like to find out more *about* being Jewish."

The minister did not seem to take this very seriously.

"Well," he said. "We know all about Jews. We have read about them in the Bible. But you are perfectly acceptable as a Christian and a good baptized and confirmed Presbyterian. Don't worry about something that has no relevance, an ancient religion. What does it really have to do with you?

"My advice is just to forget about it. You have a Christian husband, and even though he has some Jewish blood, that doesn't seem to hold him back from anything, and no one really knows about it. You also have two good Christian, baptized children, and a lovely home with real security and happiness. What else could you need? Everything in Judaism has been fulfilled in Christianity anyway. It is no longer relevant at all.

"In fact," he went on. "I have been considering making your husband an elder of the church in the next couple of years. He will be visiting members of the congregation, talking to them, even preaching a sermon or two."

Feeling that this surely would solve all their problems, he got up, smiling. "I really have to run along now . . . other people to visit. Oh, we do miss your dear mother. Such an angel. What a saint! And to think she found a poor abandoned child and brought her up and made her a Christian."

With the smile still on his face, he went out.

There was silence in the room for several minutes, and then Dorothy turned to Richard. "I just can't accept what he said. It kind of gnaws at me, at my very being. Who am I? Where do I come from? Am I Jewish? What does it mean to be Jewish? In fact, I don't think I have ever seen a real Jew. Do you think there are any in Bradford?"

Richard had become very agitated. "I doubt it," he said. "And we mustn't let people know." He hesitated. "Dorothy," he said at last. "I never told you what happened to me at school. Not here in Bradford, but in Selcourt, where we lived until I was fourteen. One of the boys found out about my mother being Jewish. He told the other boys, and they started calling me names and mocking me. I cannot describe to you what that did to me, the effect it had on me.

"I couldn't tell my mother and father about it because it would have hurt and upset them. It only lasted for a few days because even in those days I was bigger and stronger than the other boys in my class.

"I went to the boy who had started the rumor and threatened him with all kinds of things. I was surprised at myself because I had never done anything like that before or since. He actually became very frightened and told our classmates he had made up the story about my mother just to see what I would do. The situation calmed down after a few days, but I had to threaten a few more boys in the class. I can't begin to tell you what a terrible experience that was. Everyone just gangs up on you and you can't do anything.

"I can't see our kids going through something like that. I just can't. I know my mother couldn't help being Jewish, but there were moments when I actually felt I hated her for that. At the same time, of course, I loved her."

Dorothy had become very quiet. "Are you going to hate me if you find out I am Jewish?" she said in a low voice.

"Of course not! How can you say that?" shouted Richard. "How would anyone know?"

Dorothy remained quiet.

"Look, Dorothy," Richard went on. "You can read books and read as much as you like about Jews and Judaism, but please don't speak to people. Please don't let it get out. Please don't tell anyone anything."

"I would like to find out," said Dorothy, simply.

"Yes, read, read whatever you like, but don't look at it as so important. Religion is good in its place, but it starts becoming too much if it interferes in a person's personal life. We have been happy. We are happy, aren't we?"

He had been shouting up to this point, but now he became quiet, almost boyish and pleading. Dorothy had hardly said a word. He wasn't a person who shouted. He was, in general, a good-natured, placid person. It affected her deeply to see him so angry and upset.

"That's fine, Richard, that's fine. I won't tell anyone, at the moment anyway. But I do want to read books. Perhaps I will get some from the library. They can order them on inter-library loan."

"What will they think?" asked Richard. "This is the kind of town where everyone knows everyone else."

"Who cares what they will think?" said Dorothy, suddenly becoming angry. "Why must we live our lives according to what people will think?"

"Dorothy," pleaded Richard. "We have a good name in this town. People like us. If it came out that we had Jewish connections, who knows what might happen? Please Dorothy, do this discreetly. You can look for your family, but please leave this Jewish thing out of it. Aren't we happy being Christians?"

Dorothy suddenly became thoughtful. "Didn't you ever have doubts?" she asked.

"Yes, I suppose I did, as a teenager. I got sort of tied up

with the idea that maybe one shouldn't worship anyone else but the Creator, but then I stopped getting involved with all that and concentrated on football."

"I had doubts," said Dorothy. "I even discussed them with Rev. Purdy."

She had, indeed, had long discussions with him as a teenager, strangely enough on the same lines as Richard had had his doubts. She had questioned, among other things, why Christianity had had to come into being at all. Why couldn't a person just relate to the Creator, as was written in the Old Testament? The minister had told her about a blood sacrifice which was necessary for atonement and forgiveness as the Temple did not stand, but she had pointed out that in the Bible there were seventy years between the first and second Temples when there had been no blood sacrifice, and none of the books which had been written then had cried about the idea that the Creator could no longer be approached because no forgiveness was available.

She had been reading the Book of Esther which had been written when there was no Temple standing. During that time the whole Jewish nation had returned to the Creator in complete repentance, with no blood sacrifices. Her minister had spent several sessions with her until he had eventually complained to her parents and they had intervened and asked her not to ask questions. She had complied, but had never really been satisfied. She thought about this now.

Rev. Purdy started to visit them fairly regularly, as he felt, and was told by Richard, that Dorothy was beginning to overreact to her mother's last words, to stir, and to make a fuss about things where it wasn't necessary. Perhaps he even remembered her earlier doubts.

On one occasion, he asked her if her interest was truly in

her Jewish roots or if it was rather a drive to find her natural family. "Many adopted children have a great deal of curiosity about their biological family, but they usually learn that their adoptive family are the ones who really cared and care for them. Your adoptive parents were real saints. You wouldn't want to hurt them, would you?"

"No, no," said Dorothy, suddenly feeling guilty. How could she be asking all these questions? But then she remembered. Her mother had kept the star of David and had given it to her, stressing that it was a Jewish star of David.

Her mother would have understood.

Seeing that he was not gaining ground, the minister walked in one day with a book, written by one of his colleagues. It was a study on anti-Semitism.

"I have brought you a book," he said. "It will make you realize that digging up Jewish roots can only lead to trouble. People *hide* their Jewishness. Jews are different. They can't mix with others, and people persecute them. By reading this one can see why. It goes into a study of the Second World War, and also gives a history of anti-Semitism.

"Being Jewish will just complicate your life. It isn't worth it. Read this book and you will see. I am sorry I have to show you what a cruel and dangerous heritage you might have had. You will learn to thank Heaven that you and your children are completely out of it. See what you might have exposed your children to? These innocent Christian children."

Richard had turned white. He looked at Dorothy, anger suddenly blazing. "I told you," he said. "I told you. We are just going to forget this whole thing. What does it matter, anyway? You don't know your family, your real family. They think that you were killed in the train crash. Why should you stir things up and ruin us all? Especially our innocent Christian children!"

ON A GOLDEN CHAIN

Rev. Purdy tried to hide a smile which had crossed his face. "This is just causing trouble between the two of you, Dorothy," he said. "Try to forget about it."

"Forget my real family?" said Dorothy. "Perhaps they have been searching for me all these years. I want them. I want to see who they are, where they come from. Don't you understand?"

"I don't know where you will begin to look," said Rev. Purdy, shrugging his shoulders. "But I suppose you can try, as long as you don't go into the Jewish thing too much."

Richard nodded in sullen agreement. "She won't find them, anyway," he said, under his breath.

CHAPTER

6

The station master looked puzzled. "I am not sure where you would really start to look." A train crash around twenty-three years ago? Far away, possibly not even in this country?

"I suppose there must be some way of tracing it. There aren't *that* many train crashes, thank Heaven. It was just so long ago." Suddenly, his face brightened. "Yes, yes, of course. How could I forget? The time is exactly right. Everyone knew about it in those days. It was a famous train crash in the South of England. In Cornwall somewhere, or Devonshire. Where was it again? A big tragedy it was, a really big tragedy. I remember hearing all the details. My father knew more about it. He was on the railways at the time. It was something to do with a mix up with the signals. It was really terrible. There were many people killed and scores injured. It was in Southbroom. The Great Southbroom Train Crash. Nothing like that had ever happened near there before or since. The newspapers went on and on about it."

"How could we find out more about it?" Dorothy asked. "Who would really know?"

The station master was thoughtful. "I know who would," he said at last. "In London there is a Railway Museum. The curator there has, all his life, been fascinated by trains. He might be able to tell you more about it. He knows about every model of train, how each one is different, where they are made and even who some of their drivers were and which lines they were responsible for."

"How do we get in touch with him?" asked Dorothy.

"Well," said the station master, picking up a Railway Journal. "The number of the museum is always here." He found it and gave them the number, asking them to be sure to ask for Mr. Joe Blackman.

They phoned the number as soon as they returned home and were mildly disappointed to learn that Mr. Blackman would only be in the next day. He was in the next morning, however, and Dorothy spoke to him, asking for as much detail as possible about the Great Southbroom Train Crash.

"We actually have a whole section on the crash at the Railway Museum," he said. "If you are ever over this way you should come see it. I have photographs, newspaper cuttings and pictures of the bridge."

"The bridge?" asked Dorothy.

"Yes," said the curator. "That's how the crash occurred. It was a single line bridge. That means that two trains could not cross it at the same time. There had to be a very exact synchronization of signals. Something went very wrong, Two trains tried to cross the bridge together—obviously . . ."

Dorothy did not even like to think of what had happened.

The curator continued. "Almost everyone in the front two coaches of both trains was killed. Those coaches just crumpled and fell into the water. The passengers didn't have a chance, no chance at all. Many others were also killed and scores, I would say, hundreds, were injured. It was like a battleground, perhaps even worse than a battleground.

"But you must come see the pictures. One day, when you are in the city, I'll show them to you. I also have the newspaper clippings. I will show you everything. Perhaps you could tell me when you would be coming and I'll be sure to be available to you."

"It will be soon, very soon," said Dorothy. "I will contact you." She put down the phone and said, "Southbroom." Perhaps we should even go there, she thought. She waited for her husband to return to share the news with him.

Feeling somewhat guilty about his outburst after Rev. Purdy's last visit Richard agreed rather quickly to a visit to the city to see the museum.

"Are you sure it's Southbroom?" he asked.

Dorothy looked confused. "Well, that seems to be it," she said. "The timing is more or less right and it is several hundred kilometers away. Where else could it be? We haven't found any papers indicating where my parents grew up or where they lived. There must be some, somewhere!"

In the weeks following her mother's death, Dorothy had realized how little she knew not only about her own, possibly Jewish origins, but even about the background of her adoptive parents. Very few of her parents' important papers had been found, and certain vital ones, such as birth certificates, were missing.

On the other hand, she had not really been through all their things. She had started to pack up the cottage, but she

ON A GOLDEN CHAIN

felt she needed a few days break from it. It just held too many memories. However, she realized that she just *had* to find some papers, or in some way find out who she really was. There must be a way of finding out, even without papers.

She decided to search the cottage again and pack some more of her mother's things. As she entered the familiar gate, she experienced the sudden sense of loneliness which had descended on her so often after her mother's death. She had been so close to her parents, but, in view of what her mother had told her, had she ever really known her parents? She tried to remember what she knew about their background, what they had told her. It had been surprisingly little.

She unlocked the door and stepped into the silent cottage, which was already beginning to become quite musty. She quickly opened the windows, and as the fresh breeze came in, she started to feel better. She had brought some boxes and suitcases with her, and she went back to the car to fetch the rest of them. She should have brought a friend with her to help her, but perhaps it was better without anyone. She had not told any of her friends about what her mother had told her. They were all settled in their community, apparently happy and content. They would not understand.

She packed her mother's dresses one by one into the suitcases. Each one held special memories for her, and she tried to steel herself as she did this by forcing herself to think of nothing. After about ten minutes, she decided she could pack up only with Richard and the children present. She could not do it alone.

A storm was coming up, and the wind began to whistle through the half-empty house. She shut the windows. Should she leave? She decided, however, that since she was there she would try once more to look through the papers. Her parents had kept all kinds of unimportant papers—telephone bills from years ago, the dog license for old Paddy who had died when she was still a child. So many papers, and yet nothing from the time before she was five years old. But *she* surely had papers. What about her birth certificate? She had to produce that when she was married. She remembered that she had an abridged copy of it, but she was sure it had indicated her place of birth as this town and her parents as her parents. She would write away to the relevant government department to obtain the complete certificate. That in itself would sort out some of the problems.

She picked up the two photograph albums which showed many pictures of herself in various settings— at the beach, at her sixth birthday party, at a fancy-dress party, at Sunday school, at Christmas, Easter, and so on.

There were photographs taken with her parents, with the dog, outside the house, inside the house. She had occasionally wondered, especially when she was a child, why there had been no baby pictures of herself and her parents. When she had asked, her father or mother had usually looked around vaguely and said, "They are not in *this* album." Now she understood. At the time, she had searched and searched, but now she realized that there never had been another, earlier album.

It was becoming dark. Surely she could not have been in the cottage for so long. No, it was the weather. The clouds outside were becoming darker and darker. She had better hurry, otherwise she could be caught in a terrible storm.

Surely there must be *some* papers that were relevant. Not to herself–she understood that. Even her parents didn't know who she really was, but surely she could find something relating to them, at least, and to their birth date, or to the place they grew up, or perhaps to the place where they were living when they found her. And who were her real parents?

Were they still alive? Maybe she wasn't an orphan at all. Maybe she had brothers and sisters, and her children would have cousins. Jewish cousins.

She resolved then that whatever happened, she would fully investigate her own Jewish roots and do everything in her power to trace her family. She would have to be extremely careful as far as Richard was concerned. The last thing in the world she wanted to do was cause serious friction in her marriage and in her family.

And with that, she let herself out of the cottage and drove home.

Richard looked up from his newspaper with an expression on his face which showed he had been far more within his own thoughts than reading the paper.

"You know, Dorothy," he said as she walked in, "I've been reading some of those things on anti-Semitism in the book Rev. Purdy lent us. I want you to read it, too. I want you to see what a curse it is to be Jewish. But there is something in that book, something quite incredible."

"I *have* been reading the book, and ever since, I've felt I somehow want to find out more about Jewish people," said Dorothy, interrupting him. "I wasn't aware of the pogroms and persecutions. I mean, you hear about it a little, but I never had any glimmer of what it meant, what was happening all over. Rev. Purdy wanted to put me off, but these are my people. Maybe, during the war, some of my relatives died in the gas chambers. Who knows? I just *have* to know."

Richard nodded. Dorothy was amazed and a little wary at her husband's change in attitude, especially as a result of reading such a book.

"Dorothy," said Richard. "Jews have been dying through the ages. Maybe they really had something worth dying for."

Dorothy was silent. What about Richard's anger, his fears for the children? She would have thought a study on anti-Semitism wold have made it worse, as was obviously Rev. Purdy's intention.

"Perhaps, Dorothy, we should speak to someone and find out just a little. When you go into the city to see the railway museum, we should arrange to see a minister or a rabbi and just speak to him. There are no Jews here in Bradford, I am sure, and anyway, it wouldn't be good for anyone to know." The old fears were returning. "We don't have to give our name or anything. We could just go and speak to him, just to find out a little, only once, of course, and then we can read up on the subject. Do you think there are Jews in London?"

"There will be lots of them, I'm sure," said Dorothy. "We could phone and make an appointment. You could take a day off work and we could organize everything. In fact, I'll do it now," she added quickly before Richard could change his mind.

She picked up the London Telephone Directory, opened it at random and then stared at it vaguely.

"Whom do I phone?" she said at last.

"A rabbi. We want to speak to a rabbi, don't we?" asked Richard.

"Yes, but I mean, what do I look up?" she asked.

"Jews, or Jewish, I suppose," he replied, becoming aware of her problem. "I suppose there must be something Jewish in the book."

She obediently turned the pages. There were, in fact, a few Jewish organizations to choose from.

"It doesn't say rabbi or anything, but I'll phone this number," she said. "Jewish Women's Benevolent Fund. They should be able to tell me how to find a rabbi."

She found herself speaking to an efficient receptionist

who immediately provided her with the names and telephone numbers of some rabbis. She had marked R, O or C next to each name as the woman had mentioned whether each one was Reform, Orthodox or Conservative.

"What's the difference?" Richard asked.

Dorothy explained that she hadn't really wanted to ask the receptionist that question, because the receptionist had assumed that she knew.

"All right," said Richard. "Try Reform. It sounds most like Presbyterian—the Reformation and everything."

Dorothy dialed a number. There was no reply. She dialed a second number, but put down the receiver when she got the busy signal.

"Try Orthodox this time," said Richard, seeing that she was not being successful. "There are a few numbers here. Let's try this one, Rabbi Yosef Kessler."

Dorothy dialed the number and was soon put through to Mrs. Sara Kessler who explained that her husband was not home. He would be back within the hour. Could she be of any help?

Introducing herself as Mrs. Dorothy Smith, she told her briefly what had been happening over the last few days, watching Richard's face whitening with anxiety at the thought of what they were doing. Why had he started this?

"My husband will be home very soon," Mrs. Kessler said. "And I am sure he would be very interested to speak to you. How long would it take to drive over?"

"Drive over, now?" said Dorothy. She hadn't thought of that. It shouldn't take more than ninety minutes if Richard kept up speed, but the weather wasn't good. She looked at Richard. He had gone a beet red. He wanted to tell Dorothy to put down the phone and forget about it, but perhaps it was better to get it over and done with forever.

But what about the children? "The children," he whispered.

"They can come too," she said. "They will sleep in the car on the journey there and back."

Reading the urgency in Dorothy's eyes, Richard agreed.

"Well, Mrs. Kessler, I'm not sure where we could leave our children on such short notice," Dorothy began.

"They can sleep in one of our children's rooms if they are tired when they come. No problem at all."

"Then we will come," said Dorothy and quickly took down the address.

"I have a feeling that we have just gotten ourselves into something we might not be able to get out of," said Richard. "Maybe just phone and cancel, or . . . oh, all right, let's go. Maybe only *you* should speak to him."

CHAPTER 7

Some two hours later, a wet car, its windshield wipers battling the last drops of rain, drove into the city.

As they drove into the Jewish area and saw men walking around in *yarmulkas* or black hats and long black coats, Dorothy suddenly started feeling very strange. She felt faint and giddy, as if something inside of her had become deeply shocked.

She could not explain why she was feeling this way. Perhaps the drive had been too much for her, with the wind and the heavy rain. Perhaps it was delayed shock from her mother's death.

She looked at Richard. He was hunched up behind the steering wheel, driving with a tense, sullen expression. What did he think of all this?

ON A GOLDEN CHAIN

They were approaching Rabbi Kessler's home and they stopped outside it.

"You can go in with the kids," said Richard. "I will stay outside. Please don't be long."

"You can't do that," said Dorothy. "We said we were both coming."

"Can't you see that this place is totally strange and foreign, full of odd people?" He almost wished he hadn't read the book on anti-Semitism. Now the whole project seemed like total madness. "What would anyone say if they saw us here?"

"Well, there *is* no one else around to see us, certainly no one we know," said Dorothy.

Richard realized this. Who would or could be here from Bradford who would know him?

"Well, let's just get this over with," he said as he started to get out of the car.

The children woke up and walked sleepily towards the door, which was opened by a boy about Steven's age and a girl a little younger than Lucy. Steven and Lucy became more alert.

"I'm Shlomo and this is my sister Bluma," said the boy.

"Good evening," said Richard. "We have come to see your parents."

Rabbi Kessler, a tall man with jet black hair and beard, came to the door. "Please come in," he said in a soft Israeli accent. "We have been waiting for you. Sara Chanah, my wife, told me all about you. Why don't we sit down and chat? I was afraid the storm would turn you back."

He led them into the living room and was joined by his wife, who asked them if they had had supper. Dorothy suddenly remembered that she hadn't. She hadn't even thought of it. Here she was, starving her family!

"I hope you haven't eaten yet," the rabbi continued, noticing the expression on Dorothy's face. "We just assumed you hadn't and prepared for you. Please join us."

Steven and Lucy had disappeared somewhere with Shlomo and Bluma, followed by their younger sister Rivkie, and the smallest child Levi.

Three older children came into the room.

"I'd like you to meet my older children Moshe, Leah and Dina," said Mrs. Kessler. "But come, we will eat."

Two hours later, after they had eaten supper and been chatting in the living room over some coffee, even Richard felt strangely, though reluctantly, at home.

Rabbi Kessler was very different from the Rev. Ian Purdy. He seemed to enjoy being asked questions, and not to resent or brush over them. They felt, in many ways, that they had somehow known him for years and were able to talk very freely with him.

"One thing is definite," he said, looking at Richard. "*You* are Jewish."

"Me?" said Richard suddenly feeling sick. "I know I am partly Jewish, but I have mostly Christian blood."

"Every drop of your blood is Jewish," said Rabbi Kessler. "Jewishness goes according to the mother, no matter *who* your father was or who your mother's father was. You are definitely and absolutely Jewish."

Richard turned a little white as he digested this.

Turning to Dorothy, Rabbi Kessler said, "As far as you, Mrs. Smith, it is very likely you are Jewish, highly likely, but we have to prove it, for your sake and your children's sake. If we can't prove it, we have to go to the *beis din* and see what can be done. In the meantime we have to let you both know what Judaism is all about."

At that moment, little Rivkie came in to say good night to her parents.

"Say *shema* before you go to bed," said her father.

The child spontaneously covered her eyes with her right hand.

"*Shema Yisroel, Hashem Elokeinu, Hashem* . . ." There was a pause.

"*Echod,*" Dorothy said suddenly.

"*Echod,*" Rivkie repeated.

Rabbi Kessler was smiling. "How did you know that?" he asked. "You didn't learn that at Sunday school."

"I don't know," said Dorothy. "But when Rivkie said it, I knew that I knew it. What does it mean?"

"We are affirming that there is one G-d, who is the Creator and Sustainer of the Universe. Only one, and no other," said the rabbi. "Over the years, Jews have gone to their death saying these words rather than adopt another faith."

"I read about that," said Dorothy. "Rev. Purdy gave us a book to read about anti-Semitism, and I read about it."

They spoke for almost three hours more until Dorothy looked at her watch in horror. "How could we take up so much of your time?" she asked.

"It's quite late," the rabbi agreed. "But we are often late like this, much later, in fact. Your children seem to be fairly comfortably asleep, so why the rush?"

And so the discussion continued. "What are you doing to trace your family?" the rabbi asked.

Dorothy explained what she had tried to do, and that she was going to try to obtain her complete birth certificate. For some reason, she said nothing about the Southbroom crash.

"Did you have any other recurring dreams or nightmares?" he asked.

"Not really," said Dorothy. "Oh yes, there was another

one, a strange one. But it isn't relevant, I am sure. It was a sort of 'Alice Through the Looking Glass' one. I would be a child and I would be standing in front of a mirror looking at myself, and then . . . it sounds so strange! But after all, it's only a dream. And then the reflection of myself would step out of the mirror and I would be standing with my reflection looking out of the window. Crazy, isn't it? But I would dream this very often. In fact, I still do."

"You mentioned a similar kind of thing in your nightmare about the train," said the rabbi. "You would be standing looking into your own reflection, as it were, lying on the platform covered in blood."

"Yes, I suppose it is similar," said Dorothy.

She suddenly felt overwhelmingly tired. The rabbi noticed this and looked at his watch.

"When can you come back and talk to us again?" he asked. "Perhaps you should be with us for one *Shabbos*. But not yet. Maybe we could get together regularly. We should get together for a *shiur*—a study session—once a week."

"Not right now," said Richard, suddenly remembering his antagonism. Did he really want this? Of course not! He? Richard? Jewish! There must be some mistake. He must leave the house with his wife and family and never come back! Never ever must he come back!

It had been fascinating talking to the rabbi and time had flown, but he didn't want to be Jewish . . . no way!

"I'm very busy at work these days," Richard said. "Perhaps when things settle down. I will contact you."

"You have my number. Please call any time," said the rabbi. "And here are the books you wanted to borrow." He put them into Richard's hands.

He helped them bring their sleeping children to the car and wished them a safe journey.

As he re-entered the house, Sara Chanah, his wife, came to him. "It is way past two a.m.," she said.

"I know," the rabbi answered. "I know. But these people are Jews, I am sure, and their children are Jews, and they have everything stacked against them. They have been brought up as Christians. Their friends are Christian. They live in a town where there isn't another Jew. It is going to be so difficult. I had to somehow make a mark on them. She is interested to find out. He is interested, but at the same time he is antagonistic and afraid. But I had to show them the beauty of *Yiddishkeit*, something that would make them persist against all odds."

"I know," said Sara Chanah. "I know . . . I understand."

The rabbi picked up a *sefer* and began to learn, and his wife left him undisturbed.

CHAPTER

8

Dorothy ran from the garden into the house. The phone was ringing. It had probably been ringing for some time.

She hoped the person would carry on ringing. So often, as she arrived at the phone and stretched out to pick it up, the ringing would stop. This time, it didn't.

"Good morning, Mrs. Wilson." The voice sounded official. She listened for a few moments, wrote down an address and put down the phone, her hands trembling. It had been about her abridged birth certificate which she had sent in, requesting a complete copy in the hopes of finding out more about herself and her parents. There was something wrong with the registration, the number, the whole certificate. In fact, it seemed that either there was some mistake or else the thing was a masterpiece in forgery. She had to go to a government office in the city to rectify this.

She had known this, hadn't she? But nevertheless it was a shock, a big shock. A forgery! Apart from this there was no way of gaining more information about her parents.

The government official had asked her to bring all her other papers, any papers which might be relevant, especially her baptismal certificate. How could she have had one? And they wanted her to come within the week. That would give her until next Thursday! What would happen? They would have to set up some sort of investigation. But that was what she wanted, wasn't it?

A wave of doubt suddenly overcame her. She was busy burning familiar bridges, cutting away at the heritage her adoptive parents had given her, disrupting her husband's and children's lives. She felt a lot of guilt about having stirred up the "Jewish thing."

Since their visit to Rabbi Kessler, Richard's antagonism had been replaced by a black depression. He seldom smiled and even avoided going to the gym, which for him was extremely unusual under any circumstances.

Besides feeling shocked and ashamed of being completely Jewish, Richard had been devastated by Rabbi Kessler's brief introduction to *Shabbos* observance.

It would completely destroy his sports life. Almost all the matches took place on a Saturday. It was a Christian country, after all. Surely no one could expect a person to give up his sports activities. These were necessary to keep fit. These were necessary for living.

Dorothy had realized this. She, too, was both attracted and frightened by what Rabbi Kessler had told them. They would send back the books they had borrowed, without, of course, giving a return address. She had also requested some books from the library, indicating that she was doing some research.

But her husband was Jewish, one hundred percent Jewish. The rabbi had said so. He had asked, in fact, if he could look through his mother's papers to obtain certain details. He had found everything with little difficulty. That meant that Lucy and Steven had another stronger, deeper Jewish heritage.

Sunday dawned, and with it, an emptiness. They should all be in church, shouldn't they? What would Rev. Purdy think if they didn't come? Neither Richard nor she had even considered telling Rev. Purdy about their meeting and discussion with Rabbi Kessler. They felt he would not approve or understand. She heard the children looking through their drawers.

"I'm going to wear this for Sunday school," Lucy was saying. "And you must wear your blue suit. It goes with your new shirt."

The doubts returned. What was she doing to the children? They were so happy and settled in the life they had now. There was nothing wrong. They had friends. Perhaps she should just forget everything and continue as if nothing had happened.

She found herself automatically dressing for church, a kind of black heaviness enveloping her. She heard Richard's voice. "What are you dressing up for? Are we going to church?"

"Yes," said Dorothy suddenly feeling cold. "Yes, this is where we belong. I don't want to stir things. Rev. Purdy was right. This is where we belong."

"But Rabbi Kessler," he began.

"We will cancel it," she said. "I can't take it . . . I can't."

"Then I will come with you. You can't go alone," he said, feeling a strange mixture of relief and disappointment. But had they ever agreed not to go to church?

And so it was that the Wilson family attended church that Sunday. They had no idea—or perhaps they did have *some* idea—that this would be the last time they would ever attend a church of any description.

"I don't belong there any more," said Dorothy as the family gathered around the lunch table after church. "I feel in a way that I don't belong anywhere. I kept thinking about all the things Rabbi Kessler said. I couldn't even sing the hymns. The words just stuck in my throat. I kept getting a picture in my mind of Rabbi Kessler."

Richard nodded. He had felt the same way, but at the same time he didn't want to break with Rev. Purdy and the church. He felt a wave of self-pity wash over and engulf him. They had been so happy and contented! Why had all this happened to them?

He knew his wife, and he knew that for her there was no real turning back. But he was the one who was Jewish. Rabbi Kessler had said that. But Rev. Purdy had said that he wasn't, that he only had some Jewish blood.

"Dorothy," he said. "At the rate you are going we won't be able to stay in this village. We can't leave now, I know," he said, as he saw her start. "But in a few years time we will have to move somewhere else."

Steven suddenly became excited. "Can we go and live near Shlomo Kessler? And Bluma? And Rivkie? And Levi? We could play with them every day!"

Dorothy, who had been thinking of the effect they were having on their children by leaving the church, suddenly laughed.

"You liked them?" she asked.

"Oh yes," said Lucy. "They were the bestest . . . the very bestest."

The rest of the day was spent with the whole family packing up Dorothy's mother's cottage. They had decided to adopt much of the furniture. The rest had to be sold to whomever would want to buy it. Then, they would sell the house. According to the will, Dorothy was the sole heir. They had put the estate in the hands of a lawyer in the city.

Perhaps he could help. Perhaps he could find out more about her parents' background. She decided to arrange to see him on Wednesday when she went to the department about her birth certificate. She had also made arrangements with the curator of the railway museum. He would show them everything he had about the Southbroom tragedy.

She stood on a chair and unhooked her mother's curtains. These wouldn't really fit the windows of her house, but maybe one day they would move. Not yet, but some time. She would keep them. They were lovely curtains and held such precious memories. She would wash them and pack them away.

CHAPTER 9

The government official looked doubtfully at Dorothy and Richard and then at the two children. Their marriage certificate seemed to be in order. That *must* be valid. Their children had legal birth certificates. But Mrs. Dorothy Wilson? Something was very strange about her birth certificate. Strange that the computer hadn't picked it up. But they hadn't had computers in those days. This was definitely not in order, not in order at all!

"This is your exact birth date, isn't it?" he asked again. "April 2, 1958."

Dorothy sighed. "I can probably say with just about a hundred percent certainty that it isn't. I have told you what my mother told me. How could she have known my birthday?"

The official shook his head again. "This is

highly irregular, highly irregular. In fact, it is a crime!"

"Whom are you going to charge? My parents?" asked Dorothy, patiently.

"Where are your parents' birth certificates?" he asked again.

"You should be giving us a death certificate soon," she said.

He seemed to remember something, requested the date and went to the computer. "Actually, we have the death certificate ready, but much of the information requested comes up as 'not available.' "

He then looked for her father's death certificate, with similar responses of 'pending' and 'not available'.

"Well," he said at last. "You are not registered."

"You mean, I don't *exist*?" asked Dorothy, beginning to feel quite amused.

The official looked at her doubtfully. "Oh, you do, but you had better see a lawyer and see that you do officially."

"We are actually going to one right away," said Dorothy.

The lawyer seemed far less flustered by the problem. "Of course we will fix it up," he said. "You have been in this country for years. We can get proof of that. You are married and have two children, and I have been going through the will you handed over to me earlier. You are going to be quite a wealthy young woman. Besides the house, the will gives you access to a safe deposit box. I opened it, as you know, with your permission and have found a considerable number of share certificates, but no documents, I am afraid. I mean, not the kind you are looking for. But I am sure we can manage something. You certainly have the finances to conduct a full investigation, if you wish to do so."

Dorothy was baffled. Though the family had been comfortable, she had never for one moment even considered that they were wealthy. The news, though pleasant, suddenly gave her a headache.

Being in London again, even though they were nowhere near Stamford Hill, made Dorothy think more strongly about the Kesslers. She had found it extremely difficult to put them out of her mind. One part of Rabbi Kessler's discussion with them in particular kept on coming back to her, invading her thoughts.

Rabbi Kessler had begun by explaining that in Judaism there are many laws or *mitzvos*. However, we are aware of the reasons or part of the reasons only for some of these, so we have to accept that these *mitzvos* or commandments came from a Commander, Hashem. We do them because they are G-d's command, rather than because we understand each one of them. He also explained that, according to some views, the word *mitzvah* is derived from the word *tzavsa*, meaning attachment, and that by doing the *mitzvos*, one attaches oneself to Hashem. He explained that in accepting Hashem as Commander, the doing of the commandments would follow automatically, because they had their source in great and deep levels, beyond anyone's comprehension. By doing *mitzvos*, explained the rabbi, they would come to understand and to find a depth and significance in their actions.

"Take it slowly," he had said. "It will come to you."

As they approached the Railway Museum, Steven and Lucy gave a whoop of delight to see a shiny steam engine standing majestically in front of the entrance.

They were twenty minutes earlier than expected and the curator was not yet ready for them, so Richard and Dorothy went around with the excited children, admiring the many exhibits. Dorothy felt quite surprised that she didn't have her usual sick feeling when she saw a train. With some difficulty,

ON A GOLDEN CHAIN

Richard persuaded Dorothy not to go immediately to the Southbroom exhibit. He wanted her to see it as the curator presented it.

On the east side of the museum was a mural depicting one of the first trains, with the people standing in open trucks. The engine had been made by George Stevenson himself.

They saw pictures of the suspension railway from South America, the German overhead railway, the Swiss rack railway, the South African articulated steam locomotive and the Australian, American and Canadian trains pulled by diesel and electric locomotives.

They paused a long time looking at a chart of various wheel arrangements and of the head codes used to distinguish the type of train.

There were several other engines in the museum, one of which was obviously set aside for children to climb on. There were also several coaches, a dining car and a freight car.

The museum included several small exhibits, station lamps, dinner gongs, antique milk jugs and tea pots, and various uniforms. There were ticket machines and train-labels.

At the far end was a compete section on signals, showing the old signal boxes. It was obvious that with these signals, some grave mistakes could have been made.

Dorothy looked at her watch just in time to see the curator walk into the museum. He immediately took them to the Southbroom exhibit.

Dorothy felt she might faint as she looked at the twisted metal, half falling over the bridge, following whole pieces of the front carriages which had obviously already gone over. The pictures were all too real. She knew that kind of picture from her dreams. Not that a bridge had ever appeared in her dream, but that was probably irrelevant. Was this the train

ON A GOLDEN CHAIN

crash which had haunted her for so long?

She looked at the newspaper cuttings which had in fact gone on and on, only thinning out after several weeks.

Many complete families had been killed along with the others. Was her family among them? Did they have Jewish names? There was no real way of telling. Some of the more badly wounded were named. Perhaps, among these, were the names of her parents. But how was she to know?

There was only one way . . . only one way!

CHAPTER 10

"Richard, would it be possible for you to take a couple of weeks' leave?" Dorothy asked a few days later. "We need a break, all of us. We could go down South . . ."

"To Southbroom," Richard finished her sentence with a half-smile.

Dorothy laughed. "That's right. We can see the site of the train crash and talk to the people there and try to find the forest. Perhaps we may even be able to find out something about my parents. They must have been living in Southbroom."

"That's true," said Richard. "I never really thought of that. And maybe you will find another Rabbi Kessler and talk to him?" His voice had become slightly acid.

"Richard," said Dorothy. "Lately I have been

reading quite a bit. As we know already, Orthodoxy isn't the only Jewish way. There is Reform and Conservative. There must be those kind of Jews there, and they are different from Orthodox, not so strict, more like Presbyterian. Perhaps we could go to a service or something there and speak to the rabbis or reverends or whatever they are."

"Dorothy," said Richard patiently. "It is nearly Christmas and I do have the days off between Christmas and New Year. I could take an extra week. But how can we spend Christmas going to various synagogues?"

"We haven't been going to church," said Dorothy. "What are we going to do on Christmas day? A regular Sunday isn't much. You are playing sports and you often miss church, but what if we didn't go on Christmas day? What would people say then?"

"Maybe it is a good idea to go away," said Richard, seeing the logic of her words. "Many people go on holiday. In fact, what you say about Reform and Conservative doesn't sound quite so bad. Perhaps you could give Rabbi Kessler a call and ask him if there is a Reform or Conservative synagogue in Southbroom."

Dorothy was happy, though a little nervous to do this. Though Rabbi Kessler's words had stayed with her constantly, she had made no further contact with him except to send back two of the books with a brief note.

The rabbi immediately asked them to come over again for supper.

"No," said Dorothy quickly, though everything inside of her wanted to say yes. "It is too much for us. We are going to look at Reform and at Conservative. Do you know if there are any Reform and Conservative Jews in Southbroom?"

"Southbroom?" he queried. "Down there? Are you going on holiday? For how long are you going down there?"

"Only two weeks," said Dorothy. "We don't want to be here over Christmas because we haven't been going to church, and also that seems to be the scene of the train crash."

"The Great Southbroom Train Crash?"

"You know about it?" asked Dorothy, surprised.

"We have been to the Railway Museum over here a couple of times," he said. "They have a big exhibit on it. Have you seen it?"

"Yes," said Dorothy.

"Dorothy," said the Rabbi. "I see you returned the book on the Jewish festivals to me. Do you know what festival we will be observing in a few days?"

Dorothy thought for a minute. "It must be *Chanukah*. The festival of candles and light."

"Did you read about it?" he asked.

"Yes, yes. I read about Yehudah Maccabbee and the Greeks, and how a handful of people fought a huge army and won."

"Was that the miracle of *Chanukah*?" the Rabbi asked.

"Yes," said Dorothy, a little surprised that the rabbi was speaking to her about this.

"It was one of the miracles, Dorothy, and a great miracle," said the rabbi. "But we celebrate *Chanukah* beginning on the twenty-fifth of *Kislev*, and the battle was won and the *Bais Hamikdash* regained just before that time. So what was the main miracle that we celebrate?"

"The oil," said Dorothy. "A tiny cruse of oil lasted for eight days."

"But there was other oil," said the rabbi. "There was lots of it. What was different about this one cruse of oil?"

"The seal was not broken," said Dorothy, grateful she had done her homework. Was this an exam?

The rabbi sounded pleased with that answer.

"The Greek society was very complex and, for those times, quite civilized," he said. "They wanted the Jews to become part of it, to become more like Greeks. They didn't insist that the Jews drop their traditions. They could keep these as beautiful customs, unless, of course, these traditions interfered with their everyday lives. What did the Greeks do with the oil? They didn't remove it, pour it out, add anything to it, or really disturb it in any way. They simply broke the seal which the High Priest had put on it. They broke the seal of *kedushah*, of holiness. The true objective of the Greeks was not to prevent the rekindling of the *menorah*, but rather that it be rekindled with defiled oil. They did the same with the Jewish commandments and traditions. The seal of holiness was gone. They wanted the Jews to see them as beautiful traditions, not as divine commands to be obeyed. They wanted them to see the beauty of Torah as poetry and philosophy, but essentially as a *human* creation, and as such, able to be changed and modified from time to time. They wanted to do away with the permanence and inviolability of *Shabbos, kashrus*, and the like. They didn't want to suppress Torah. They wanted the suppression of it as Hashem's Torah."

"So, going back to what you told us, it's as if the commandments were taken away from the Commander?" asked Dorothy.

"You've got it," said the rabbi. "Dorothy, hold on to that one cruse of pure oil. Please call again."

"But rabbi," Dorothy said. "What about Conservative and Reform? Are there any in Southbroom?"

"I am not sure. Probably," said Rabbi Kessler. "Remember the miracle of *Chanukah*."

Puzzled, Dorothy put down the phone. Rabbi Kessler hadn't discussed the Reform or the Conservative movements and had simply tested her knowledge on *Chanukah*. It was very confusing.

Richard had been listening, equally puzzled, to her end of the conversation. She told him what he had said.

"Probably Reform and Conservative are rival movements to his," he said. "He didn't directly want to say that you shouldn't go there, so he made meaningless conversation about something else."

"It wasn't meaningless," said Dorothy. "It was very interesting."

Arrangements were made, the car was packed, and early Tuesday morning, the Wilson family set off for Southbroom.

The children, sleepy though excited, were soon lying across one another on the back seat. It was good to be driving through the half light of pre-dawn. Both Dorothy and Richard had always loved it. If they kept up the rate at which they were going, they would arrive just in time to eat supper at the small hotel they had booked into, a few kilometers out of the center of town.

They stopped for breakfast at a roadhouse run by a Mr. Goldstein and were soon enjoying a meal of bacon and eggs with coffee, cream and hot buttered rolls.

The owner came to see if they were satisfied with what had been served. "Delicious," said Richard. "Everything tastes so fresh. Your bacon is out of this world."

"I don't eat it myself," said Mr. Goldstein. "We Jews don't. Not that I keep kosher or anything. But bacon and pork are too way out for me. It's just not right. I've got to do *something* Jewish."

"Are you Reform, then, that you don't keep kosher?" asked Dorothy.

He was a little taken aback by the question coming from such an obviously gentile family.

"No, I'm Orthodox, like my father, grandfather and great grandfather. Not that I keep to anything except to not eating pork, and I go to synagogue on *Yom Kippur*. But just because I'm not keeping something doesn't mean to say that that's the way it has to be.

"I mean, it might sound hypocritical, but I know I *should* be eating kosher, and when I go to synagogue on *Yom Kippur*, and say the confessions, I know I'm guilty, and I say to G-d that one day I might even do something about it. But at least I know that I have sinned, that G-d is listening and that He'll give me a chance for another year.

"In Reform, they don't say that eating pork is wrong. It's right. So on *Yom Kippur* you are very confused because wrong is now right, so you don't have to be sorry. But I am sure that the people there who have had any Jewish background know very well it's wrong.

"It's too confusing for me. I will remain a not-too-good Orthodox Jew. At least I know Hashem commanded things. He is the Boss around the world, so I know things are basically okay. With Reform, G-d is a kind of non-being that you can't relate to, and I have heard that some don't believe He is there at all. It is all far too complicated for me."

"I like him," said Dorothy as they returned to the car. "He has a very honest way of looking at things. He knows what is right, but he just doesn't do it."

"Isn't that being a hypocrite?" asked Richard. "I did like him, but does he know where he's at?"

"I think he knows," said Dorothy. "I like him. He leaves room to change, to advance in something. Whether he will or not is up to him."

They had driven only a few kilometers when they heard the children arguing in the back of the car.

"It's in five days' time, definitely," said Lucy. "I know it is."

ON A GOLDEN CHAIN

"No," said Steven emphatically. "It is in four days time. I have been counting for weeks. It is in four days, isn't it, Mummy?"

"Four days to what?" asked Dorothy, genuinely puzzled.

"Oh, Mummy is joking with us. She always pretends she hasn't got all our presents and our tree and our bonbons and our turkey and everything." Lucy was laughing with the excitement of anticipation.

Both Dorothy and Richard felt their hearts sinking. Had they thought the children would just forget about Christmas? How could anyone take Christmas away from a child?

CHAPTER 11

After almost an hour of darkness they spotted the lights of Southbroom becoming clearer as the car sped towards them. Richard was stiff from driving, and Dorothy felt exhausted from the seemingly endless stretches of road, trying to keep two bored, irritable children happy.

Suddenly energy returned. They were at their destination. They drove through the town to the tiny hotel which seemed at that time like an oasis in a desert.

The entrance and reception area were decorated for the holiday. A large Christmas tree with flashing lights and an angel on the top stood in one corner. The children immediately went over to it, touching the tinsel, their eyes shining.

With the help of the doorman, Richard carried their luggage up to the two adjoining rooms,

ON A GOLDEN CHAIN

Dorothy following after prying the reluctant children away from the tree.

They had intended to eat supper and go explore the city, but they were all so weary that they agreed to a dinner served in their rooms and an early night. Tomorrow was another day. It would wait.

It was not very long before the children were asleep in the next room and Richard and Dorothy sat relaxing in armchairs, drinking coffee. It felt good to be away from everyone and everything, good to be free of the household and the work responsibilities. It felt good just to be together.

They talked about many things, especially sources of conflict in their lives, namely, things connected with religion.

For the first time they were able to speak about it openly, without the usual tension which had been blighting their lives and their relationship.

Dorothy realized that Richard was as much affected by the "Jewish thing" as she was. He had been very deeply stirred by the book on anti-Semitism and he had felt an almost overpowering attraction to everything Rabbi Kessler had portrayed, to the point where he had to fight it with everything he had.

He had also felt it almost impossible to return to church. In one sense, he yearned for Judaism. In another sense, he wanted to run away and forget it ever existed. And what about his sports?

Though Dorothy was outwardly leaning more towards Judaism, she, too, admitted to very deep conflicts about it. She was not sure if that was what she wanted in life for herself and for her children. Because of Richard's antagonism she had not told him of her sleepless nights, of her poring over books, of her desperate search for an answer.

In sharing these things, they found that in actual fact they were far closer than they had imagined. Richard, too, was very eager, though apprehensive and anxious about finding Dorothy's real parents.

"Why haven't we talked like this before?" said Dorothy, suddenly. "I feel so much better, even about the points on which we disagree."

"I think we just decided to be really open with each other," said Richard. "We never really get time to do that in Bradford."

"But we have lots of time," said Dorothy.

"It's something that has to be worked on at home," said Richard, "We're both so busy that we have to make real time for communication."

The discussion returned to their religious search. "We will look at Reform and Conservative over here," said Richard. "We'll see what we can cover in two weeks. But I think I am like Mr. Goldstein. Even though I am too afraid to go near the guy, Rabbi Kessler is going to be the one for me."

They discussed the children, coming up with the very real problem of Christmas. How could you tell a child there was no more Christmas? Especially three days before. This in-between stage they were in held many problems.

"When is *Chanukah*?" asked Dorothy. "Rabbi Kessler said it was sometime soon."

"My diary has some of the Jewish holidays," said Richard. He took out the small leather-bound diary that Dorothy had given him the year before—for Christmas.

"Yes," he said. "Here it is. The first night of *Chanukah* falls on the twenty-second of December. That's tomorrow night!"

"Good," said Dorothy. "We will buy a *Chanukah menorah* and light the candles, like it said in Rabbi Kessler's book. We have eight days with Christmas sort of in the middle. We'll give them presents and money every night that we light, so that they won't even notice Christmas."

ON A GOLDEN CHAIN

The next morning, all four members of the Wilson family went shopping, first Richard and then Dorothy slipping away from the children and coming back with mysterious parcels.

Christmas, the children thought. Three, or was it four days to go?

They found the Jewish bookstore and bought a menorah and a box of gaily colored candles. Dorothy, always attracted by books, looked around.

She was fingering a book on the theology of Reform Judaism when a young man with bright, intelligent eyes and an engaging smile came up to her. "I see you are looking at one of my favorite books," he said. "I am Michael Kahn, the Reform rabbi of Southbroom. I don't recall seeing you in the Temple."

Dorothy looked at him. He was a pleasant person, indeed, but a rabbi? Not only didn't he have a beard, but he didn't have a *yarmulka*, either. She had read enough on the Reform movement to know that this was to be expected, but it still gave her a somewhat uncomfortable twinge.

"We would really like to come and talk to you, rabbi," said Dorothy. "I have been reading up on Reform."

"Only with pleasure," said the rabbi graciously and made an appointment for that afternoon.

"Call me Michael," the rabbi said almost before they could sit down. "I will call you Dorothy and Richard; and of course, Steven and Lucy." He offered the children some biscuits which he had in his office.

"Tell me about yourselves," he invited, and Dorothy proceeded to tell him the whole story about the dream, her mother, Rev. Purdy, and so on. He listened, at times making a few comments, all the time totally engrossed.

Dorothy finished, and he added part of his own story.

"My mother was a Presbyterian," he said. "My grandparents still are. She met my father who was an Orthodox Jew—not practicing, of course, but still wearing the label—and a *kohein*. They decided to marry, but the Orthodox rabbi refused to perform the ceremony even though she was willing to convert. My father wasn't going to let that kind of archaic Judaism interfere with his life, so he became Reform. My mother converted, and they got married. And here I am! A rabbi! And, what is more, my sister is also a rabbi. Up North.

"I know a lot about the Presbyterian church," he continued. "And you are not going to find the Reform Temple that different. We have done away with all the laws that are obviously out of date and inconvenient, and because we are an advancing, dynamic movement, we have been constantly bringing in new things to keep up with the times. There have also been occasions on which we have brought back things we have abolished, especially where we have seen that people have a particular attachment to them."

"Yes, I know about that," said Dorothy. "I did a lot of reading on Reform Judaism."

"Good," said Michael. "You know, then, that we feel that many things such as the kosher laws and the very strict Sabbath laws need no longer be obeyed."

"But what about G-d having commanded these things?" asked Dorothy.

"Your G-d is too small," exclaimed Michael. "We no longer have the old personal commanding G-d of Israel. We have moved to a new universal, cosmological deity who neither could nor would give specific commandments to human beings. G-d is too big, too great to be concerned if you put a piece of non-kosher meat into your mouth. Is G-d in your kitchen, prying into your pots?"

"But He is everywhere," said Dorothy. "Even in the

kitchen, and surely a G-d, who made even the tiniest things in this world in perfect detail, is great in that He is so infinitely big and yet can be concerned with the infinitely smallest detail."

"Bit of an Orthodox fundamentalist, isn't she?" said the rabbi, winking at Richard. "Come to our temple. We have services every Sunday. We changed from Saturday, because it was more convenient for everyone. It fit more into the Western world. We have an organ and a mixed choir. You wouldn't be able to tell the difference between the Temple and a Presbyterian church. In fact, last *Yom Kippur* we had so many people arriving from all over the country that we used the local Methodist church for our services and felt quite at home there. We get on well with everyone. One can hardly tell the difference between Jew and gentile. We have only a feeling of love for our fellow man. We are the answer to all you are looking for.

"In fact, you will see very little difference even theologically between the Reformed churches, those who have followed Bultman's demythologizing of their scriptures, and Reform Judaism. We don't need a heaven and hell and a spiritual world. We have to do good here in this world."

He gave the Wilsons the times of the services, fully expecting them to attend them on Sunday.

"I liked him, I really liked him," said Richard. "He had such a sense of humor and was so intelligent, though he somehow doesn't really seem Jewish. But his religion isn't for me. It just isn't Judaism. I'm not even sure if its Ethical Monotheism."

Dorothy looked at him in surprise.

"I've been reading, too," he said. "What do you think of Rabbi Michael Kahn?"

"Let's try Conservative," she said. "In fact, I asked at the book shop this morning. Friday night we can go to an Orthodox *shul*, and on Saturday morning to a Conservative one. They are both, believe it or not, in walking distance from the hotel. The Orthodox one is two streets away."

CHAPTER

12

With the urgency of having to satisfy their children for Christmas, Richard and Dorothy had, on the first days, somewhat neglected their original intention in coming to Southbroom. They had seen the railway bridge, high up as it crossed the broad, magnificent Derrich River. It was difficult to imagine that a place of such beauty could have been the scene of such a tragedy.

Dorothy thought with satisfaction of the evening before, following their first full day in Southbroom.

Using a red candle for the *shammas*, they had lit the first candle for *Chanukah*, a bright yellow one. The children had watched, intrigued, as Richard had read the blessing phonetically from a pamphlet they had been given at the shop.

ON A GOLDEN CHAIN

Their eyes opened wider, however, when they were kissed "Happy *Chanukah*" and Lucy was given a doll that crawled and Steven a realistic fire engine. They were also given money to buy something of their choice. It was explained to them that this was only the first day... seven more to go. Who could rival that?

Today was the first day of *Chanukah*, their second day in Southbroom. It was time to investigate the train crash.

They went down to the station and spoke to the station master. He was too young to have been involved with the train crash, besides which, he had not been in the area at the time. However, there was a man who was semi-retired who had had a lot to do with the crash. In fact, he had been quite ill because of it for a few years. He was in the ticket office for most of the day but would be going into the canteen for lunch at noon.

They liked Bill Temton immediately. He had graying hair, light blue eyes and looked more like a sailor than a railway man. He was more than ready to talk about the crash, despite the fact that it obviously hurt him to do so.

Had any of his family been killed? He described to them what had happened in such graphic detail that even Richard felt sick. He described half-charred people crawling around, no longer looking like human beings. He described the corpses and parts of corpses floating in the water, some bloated and black from the explosion.

He described the screaming, the moaning, the wailing—and the deathly silence. Had he been there?

Yes! He and his best friend had been on duty that day. They had both been drinking, not much, just a little. But it was strictly forbidden to drink and to go on duty, even if the smell of alcohol was disguised by peppermints, especially if one was working with the signals, as his friend was doing.

ON A GOLDEN CHAIN

People didn't actually blame his friend for the crash, though there had been an investigation. Apparently, something had gone wrong with the actual signal boxes. Perhaps something could have been done if he hadn't been drinking and he could have thought fast enough.

Dorothy was overcome with horror at the way the man had described the accident. She then went on to tell her own story, describing her dream in graphic detail.

"Doesn't sound like Southbroom," he said when she finished. "It doesn't sound like it. Though I suppose you were very young and the mind has a way of changing things. But people missing? There were plenty! Even to this day there are people missing from that crash. So many of them just went into the water and were eventually washed out to sea. They looked for the bodies for days and weeks afterwards."

"To whom can I speak who might know who is missing?" asked Richard. "I mean, how do you suggest we go about this?"

"I suppose, eventually, to the local police," said Bill. "But we have a local paper. It comes out once a week. I suggest you put in some of your story, mention where you are staying and see if anyone responds. That's one suggestion. The other is that you speak to some of the people in the town, especially the people who deal with people, like the shop owners and so on. They see and hear a lot, far more than we would ever imagine."

So, for the next couple of days, Dorothy and Richard spent their time speaking to hotel managers, shop assistants, and in fact, almost anyone who seemed to be above a certain age.

To the Wilson family, the train crash became more and more traumatic. However, they could find out nothing about either Dorothy's adoptive or her real parents.

Friday night came, and the Wilson family, leaving their three *Chanukah* candles burning in the hotel room, walked to *shul*.

It was a beautiful little *shul* with a warm community. It was the first time she had, in fact, been in a *shul*, and both she and Richard, though having to sit apart, afterwards confirmed that they had loved it. It was truly different from the Presbyterian Church. The rabbi, a young man hardly out of *yeshivah*, spoke about *Chanukah* and the importance of publicizing the miracle.

Dorothy was quite sorry she had decided to go to the Conservative synagogue the next day, but she felt she had to stick to that. It was something she had to see and experience, if only briefly.

The Conservative synagogue, usually known as the halfway house between Orthodoxy and Reform, was situated about five blocks away.

They went into the synagogue, a warm, pleasant building, and Dorothy could not see much difference between the Orthodox *shul* from the night before and this one.

From the conversation around her, Dorothy gathered that many of the people kept kosher and observed *Shabbos*, *Chanukah* and other Jewish practices. What, then, was the difference between these people and the Orthodox?

One thing which struck her, however, was that two of the choir members, young men, had driven to synagogue. Richard had later heard one of them saying to the other that they were relieved that they lived far enough away to be allowed to drive. That sounded strange, very strange.

The rabbi's speech was similar to the words of the rabbi on Friday night. He spoke about *Chanukah*, about the Hasmoneans and about the defeat of the Greeks by a handful of Jews.

ON A GOLDEN CHAIN

Everyone seemed to be so sincere, and so involved. Surely Conservative had to be the answer! It was not as extreme as Orthodox. Where necessary, the laws could be bent a little and changed somewhat. Surely this was what was needed in today's world. Both she and Richard were quite impressed. They would make arrangements and speak to the rabbi about it in the coming week.

CHAPTER 13

Breakfast in the Southbroom hotel was served twice on Sunday. The first breakfast, for those who wished to go out early, was served at the usual time. The second started at nine-thirty and went on almost until lunch time. Dorothy, Richard and the children were on the way down at ten-thirty in the morning.

As they passed the reception area, they saw that the Southbroom weekly had come out. There was Dorothy's story, on the bottom left-hand corner of the front page.

They had hardly sat down when a waiter came over to them to call her to the phone. The man on the other side sounded excited. He wanted to see her as soon as possible. He would be at their hotel in an hour.

He arrived exactly on time, a stout man with

a booming voice who kept addressing her as Brenda Geffen.

"I know it is you," he said. "Your family was in my shop every day talking to me about their five year old daughter, lost in the train crash. I saw them for close to two weeks and then, totally heartbroken, they left. Such a lovely family, but so tragically struck. And now to think that here, here you are!"

"Where are my . . . where are the Geffens?" She stammered. She could not bring herself to say the words "my parents."

"Oh, I don't know now. But all we have to do is to trace them—a nice, Reform Jewish family."

Dorothy felt oddly disappointed.

"They lived not too far away from here. They had all been on that dreadful train, but their daughter had gone with an aunt towards the front of the train to the dining car, to fetch something, just as they crossed the bridge. The aunt was killed instantly. The daughter was never found. They presumed her drowned."

"How can we contact them?" asked Dorothy, for the first time feeling strange at the thought of meeting them. What was wrong? It just was not what she had expected.

"Through the trade, probably," said the man. "They were in the men's clothing trade. I have contacts. It should only take a day or so to find out."

He got up, leaving his card. Mr. Abel Stein, 42 Worthford Road, Southbroom. Manager of Leofare Stores, 488-3339.

"But I will be in touch." And in touch he was, several times a day for the next three days. He seemed to be getting closer to his goal, and then the trail would slip through his fingers and he would begin afresh. But he never stopped looking until one day Richard commented, "It's been a whole day, Dorothy, and we have heard nothing at all from Stein."

"Do you think I haven't noticed?" said Dorothy. "My mind

is occupied with it every minute. We'll give him till tomorrow, after we see the Conservative rabbi. Perhaps he is really on to something now."

Rabbi Bronsen looked like a rabbi. He had a *yarmulka*, a trimmed beard and was surrounded by Jewish books. His shelves also contained books on psychology, philosophy, sociology, anthropology and comparative religion.

He was a pleasant man, and Dorothy looked forward to a discussion of the reconciliation of the world and traditional Judaism.

He was genuinely interested in their story and encouraging to both of them. He spoke in a scholarly way about Judaism, referring to Hashem with respect and dignity. Surely this was the answer! What could be wrong with it? Dorothy did have some questions, however.

She asked about the statement made by the choir members about being able to drive to *shul* if they lived some distance away.

The rabbi nodded in agreement.

"Traditionally," he had said, "Jews don't drive to *shul*. It is not in keeping with the spirit of *Shabbos* to be in a car. But if the person lives so far away that they can't even come to *shul*, what kind of *Shabbos* is that? So we had to allow it."

Dorothy was a little uneasy. "But it is wrong, isn't it?"

"No, no, not at all, not from that distance. We have allowed it. It is one of the things we have had to change, in order to keep the beautiful traditional spirit of *Shabbos*."

"But then anything can change," said Dorothy.

"No, no, not at all," said the rabbi. "Only where it is necessary. We treasure our heritage. We love our laws and customs and we keep to them because it holds the Jewish people together."

"But G-d made those laws!" said Dorothy. "How can you change them?"

"The laws were made to live by," said the rabbi, "And where a person cannot live a proper Jewish life any more *because* of the law, it has to be modified to suit the situation. But you will see. People in Conservative keep far more traditions than most of the people in the Orthodox *shuls*. We treasure and love our customs and traditions. We find poetry and inspiring literature in our writings, but we don't emphasize the supernatural or miraculous. We lead good, traditional Jewish lives."

Dorothy was suddenly very thoughtful. "I see," she said. "Now I understand. I understand completely."

After this, she was quiet as the rabbi spoke to them about other aspects of Conservative Judaism, wondering at the same time why his audience had become so quiet and non-questioning. Obviously, he had convinced them with his first few words.

"What made you so quiet?" asked Richard as they went into the street. "It was almost as if you switched off and went to sleep."

"I suddenly understood," said Dorothy. "I suddenly understood what Rabbi Kessler meant when he told me to hold on to that one cruse of pure oil."

She proceeded to tell him the *Chanukah* story in detail, accentuating what Rabbi Kessler had said about the defiled oil. "The Greeks didn't want the Jews to stop lighting the *menorah*. They could have poured out the pure oil or removed it. Instead, they broke the seal, and by doing that, defiled it—took the *kedushah* away from it. In the same way they didn't mind if Jews kept the Torah as long as it was not seen as an indestructible G-d-given Torah. As long as they were seen as commandments removed from a relationship to a Commander and part of Hashem himself, and therefore able to be changed if necessary, the Greeks were happy. That is what the rabbi was saying. He is lighting his *menorah* with defiled oil."

It took some time for Richard to digest this, but as soon has he did so, he agreed wholeheartedly with his wife.

"I think we should go back to Rabbi Kessler," he said at last.

Still no word from Abel Stein. They would phone him. A rather sheepish voice answered, hardly recognizable as that of Mr. Stein.

"I'm sorry," he said. "I was embarrassed to call you. I spoke to the Geffens. Their daughter was found. A week after they had left, her body was washed up far along the shore. There were things which identified her undeniably, something to do with a dental abnormality, I gather. I am really sorry. I just didn't know how to tell you."

"Thank you, thank you," said Dorothy, hardly able to keep back the tears. "Please don't feel bad. You went to so much effort for us. We appreciate it. Please don't be embarrassed."

She put down the phone, put her head in her hands and cried.

CHAPTER

14

Some say that time is elastic. In many ways, the two weeks spent in Southbroom seemed like an eternity.

Richard and Dorothy had come to a deeper understanding of one another on many levels. They had spoken, really communicated, for hours and had sorted out many aspects of their lives ranging from spiritual to financial.

Their brief encounters with Conservative and Reform were enough to make them see that these were not for them. Both agreed, somewhat reluctantly, that the answer lay with Rabbi Kessler. Both knew it would mean some drastic changes in their lifestyle and probably the loss of many friends. Both knew it would be impossible to hide their Jewish interests for much longer, and yet they hardly admitted this, even to themselves.

Despite their efforts at making *Chanukah* "better than Christmas," the children had been confused and upset on Christmas day. Christmas had been very much a focal point in their lives. It was going to take more than a little effort to depose Santa Claus and many other aspects of Christian tradition.

They had almost found Dorothy's family, except that it hadn't been her family. All along, something inside her had told her that she wasn't Brenda Geffen, and though she had been upset, at the same time she was relieved that it hadn't worked out.

However, it had strengthened her resolve to find her family. On the way back home, travelling in the car, she had been going over all the things they had done in connection with the crash, and a few words, those of Bill Temton, kept recurring in her mind. "Doesn't sound like Southbroom!" Could it be that there was *another* train crash around that time, perhaps even in a foreign country? She would ask the curator of the railway museum if he could investigate this.

They phoned the Kesslers almost immediately after they returned, and as they had almost expected, Sara Chanah invited them for supper the next day.

Rabbi Kessler asked them how their experiences had been with Reform and Conservative, and Dorothy explained how the thought of the one cruse of unspoiled oil had helped her.

He just smiled.

He started to study with them, and they were once again captivated by his words, this time, however, on a different, more committed level. Richard, however, pointed out to him at the outset that they would only be able to keep *Shabbos* up to a point. There was no way in which he could ever compromise on his sports life. Again the rabbi just smiled.

ON A GOLDEN CHAIN

Towards the end of the *shiur* he started to tell them some of the laws of *kashrus*, which, though she knew something about them, immediately caused Dorothy some panic. She had known she would have to do it one day, but already? The rabbi had said, "Take it slowly." Was this slowly?

"But," she said, "we have never done things like this. What about everything in the fridge? How would we learn everything? It's all so complicated. Where can we get kosher meat?"

"Slowly, slowly," said the rabbi. "We are only beginning. Perhaps you could start by ordering only kosher meat and not eating any other kind. You can telephone the kosher butcher, and they can deliver the order here. You can collect it every Wednesday, and write the check for me to give them."

It all sounded so simple. They would devote several sessions of study to *kashrus*. Meanwhile, they would slowly make changes in the food they were eating, provisionally dividing their existing dishes into *milchig* and *fleishig*. After about six weeks, they would buy completely new sets of dishes. They would donate their old sets to the local non-Jewish old-age home, and Rabbi Kessler would come and completely *kasher* their home, including whatever could be *kashered* of their pots, cutlery and so on. At the same time, besides the practical laws, they would be learning more about the philosophy of Judaism.

This was no vague study of superficialities. When Rabbi Kessler talked about learning and doing, he obviously meant it.

"What about the children?" Dorothy asked.

Pleased to hear the question, Rabbi Kessler said that perhaps his wife and older children could set up some *shiurim* with Lucy and Steven as well. Moshe and Leah were delighted to do this.

They had intended to learn for only two hours, but again the session stretched into hours. The children had happily fallen asleep again, and it was only in the wee hours of the morning that the Wilsons left.

It felt strange driving through the night to the town where they lived. It was almost as if they didn't belong there anymore. It suddenly looked strange and alien. Dorothy shuddered. "We can make our home fairly kosher, but we can't let it interfere with our social lives," said Richard suddenly. "However, I won't be able to eat lunch at the office any more in a few weeks. What is everyone going to think?"

"I suppose you can say you are on a strict diet, and need special food, brought from home. It would be quite true, wouldn't it?" asked Dorothy.

"But Dorothy," said Richard. "I know we want to be Orthodox and religious, but what if we really get into this thing? What if I have to go around wearing a *yarmulka* on my head all the time, like I do at the *shiur*? What would everyone say? We can't let all this really interfere with our lives. We have to live with the times. It has to suit our lifestyles. What would everyone say if I wore a *yarmulka*?"

For a few seconds Dorothy was dumbstruck. Yes, what would everyone say? In the Kessler's home everything had appeared perfectly normal, but put in the context of their town, they would stand out like sore thumbs.

For both of them the old doubts suddenly began to return. What would Rev. Purdy say when they officially left the church? What would all their friends say? They had lived all their lives in the town. Weren't they happy? The doubts were coming thick and fast. Did they really want to change their lives so drastically, to change their friends, to change their whole lifestyle? Was this what they really wanted?

"Dorothy," said Richard. "Most Jews don't keep all these

things. Most Jews, even if they go to an Orthodox *shul*, don't keep all these laws. It's just Rabbi Kessler that's different, and some of the families living in the areas around him. Most Jews do as much as they can, but they don't let it interfere too much. I mean, imagine trying to go on holiday as we went to Southbroom. We would be really restricted in where we could eat. I am sure in this modern day and age, we are not expected to keep things so strictly."

"I think we are," said Dorothy. "Everyone is supposed to."

"But nobody does," said Richard. "Or, I should say, not many people do. Do we *have* to be among the exceptions? I mean, even if we *are* supposed to be Jewish, we don't have to turn into fanatics."

Dorothy was becoming more and more agitated as she heard Richard speak. She was about to make some biting comment when she remembered that Rabbi Kessler had said nothing when Richard had told him about not giving up sports on *Shabbos*.

"Let's start with getting our home as kosher as we can and get used to that," she said. "Then we'll see what happens."

"That's okay," said Richard. "But what if Mrs. Peddelhammer wants milk with her coffee after meat or if someone brings us a cake from their home?"

"What's wrong with cake?" asked Dorothy. "What could be not kosher about cake? We can't go to that extreme."

"You'd better ask your rabbi," said Richard. "He said every ingredient in anything had to be kosher. What if they used meat fat like lard or mixed it with butter?"

Dorothy began to feel more and more depressed. Were they *crazy* to get into this? She wanted to say to Richard that perhaps they should simply refuse, never see Rabbi Kessler again and live a free life, being able to eat what they liked. She couldn't tell him this, however, because he would probably agree. Once she felt better about keeping kosher, he would be even more difficult to persuade.

"We will take it slowly," she said at last.

"And," said Richard, "I don't think we should see Rabbi Kessler too often. He has a strong influence on both of us. I feel so inspired when I am listening to him that he makes me want to change all kinds of things. I think we should cool it a little."

Dorothy smiled. Her husband seemed to have summed up the situation exactly. She, too, felt so inspired when Rabbi Kessler spoke that she felt she would be prepared to change everything. Even on the very first occasion they had met, she had felt this.

"I like to make my own decisions," said Richard. "We will go at our own pace."

"Didn't Rabbi Kessler say we would be doing that anyway?" asked Dorothy.

"Yes, he said it," said Richard, "but it's different. We can't have this religion controlling our lives. It's not normal. And we can't have Rabbi Kessler controlling our lives either. It's a free country. We don't even know for sure that you are Jewish. I mean, why get involved in all of this? Why chain yourself to six hundred and whatever laws there are? In this day and age, or in any day and age, why live a life of complete suppression? How could a G-d of love make people's lives so complicated?" His face was becoming flushed, and his eyes had become several shades darker.

Dorothy knew that this was not the time to argue or even discuss things with him. But he continued.

"Slaves, that's what we are becoming, slaves! Slaves to Hashem and slaves to Rabbi Kessler, slaves and puppets, brainless, mindless slaves and puppets!" He sat in a chair and put his head in his hands. "My mother got away from it. She moved away from all these laws and restrictions and made a new start in the gentile world. Do you know what she would have said if I had told her about this trip? She would have thought we had gone absolutely and totally crazy. What kind of people are we linking ourselves to? What kind of future are we giving our children? Let's forget about it, Dorothy! Let's just forget about it!"

Dorothy felt her eyes filling with hot tears and they started to make their way down her cheeks.

"What's the matter, Dot?" he asked, suddenly worried.

"Nothing," she said, sniffing. "I think I am allergic to something. It's nothing, just a bad cold."

"A very sudden cold," said Richard, not even remotely deceived. "I am sorry, Dot. All right, let's carry on. But we must take on *mitzvos* slowly, very, very slowly. That way there are some things we will never ever get around to doing at all, until we are very, very old."

Dorothy smiled through her tears.

"And," said Richard, "we'll start looking for your family again. There must have been another train crash. Why should it have to be in this country? Your mother said that it was far, far away. We'll find out and go after it, even if we have to follow up all kinds of train crashes. But," he said, suddenly looking serious, "what will you do if you find out you aren't Jewish? Then we can forget the whole thing!"

"But what about the star?" asked Dorothy. "The small Jewish star? The star on the golden chain?"

"Some people just wear them," said Richard.

"You know what?" said Dorothy, a look of resolution coming into her eyes. "If I found out definitely that I'm not Jewish, absolutely sure that I'm not Jewish, I think I might become Jewish!"

Richard gave a half-hearted laugh. "You're crazy," he said.

ON A GOLDEN CHAIN

"But maybe I'm crazy, too, because if you weren't Jewish, I think I would like you to become Jewish."

It was as if the sky above them had suddenly cleared.

"Let's start with the kitchen," he said.

CHAPTER 15

"Sometimes it is quite difficult to locate all these things," Mr. Blackman from the Railway Museum was saying to Dorothy on the phone. "But there was a train crash, a very catastrophic one, in a small town on the Johannesburg-Cape Town line in South Africa. Many passengers were killed, hundreds were injured, some of them very seriously.

"South Africa?" exclaimed Dorothy. "Who would have been in South Africa? It can't be that one."

Mr. Blackman went on. "There were also a few less serious train crashes around that time, one in Holland and another in Czechoslovakia. I have sent for information on all of them. I will let you have it as soon as it is available. The one in Dikbos was a very big tragedy. It must have had a great deal of newspaper coverage."

As Dorothy replaced the receiver she felt a strange sense of foreboding. Something about these places had a ring of reality. What was she going to find? Who was she? How much would she remember? Surely, she could not have come from South Africa? Were there any Jews in South Africa?

She pulled out an atlas and looked for South Africa and then for Dikbos. It didn't seem to be there, but there was Cape Town, way down south by the sea, there was Johannesburg, and there was a railway line between them. She followed it with her pen, but there was no Dikbos. The atlas was hopelessly out of date. She hadn't bought one for years, so one couldn't really tell at all. It was certainly far away, very far away.

She turned to Czechoslovakia and then to Holland, but he had not mentioned the towns, so she could not get very far.

How had her adoptive parents ended up in their town in England? And how soon after the train crash had they left wherever they had come from? It was all very confusing. What was their real name? Perhaps they had changed it.

She sighed, realizing the hopelessness of her situation. She had tried all this in Southbroom. Even if she found the train crash, how was she going to find her real family? They did not come from Dikbos. They were passing through. From where? To where? Maybe from Cape Town to Johannesburg. But they could not have lived there. Surely, they would have been on holiday.

Anyway, all one could do was to wait. She wondered how long it would take.

Dorothy and Richard had completely emptied her parents' home and had had it painted. Though it looked beautiful, it had become far more impersonal. They had advertised it for sale, and a man had responded. He would be over with his parents to look at the cottage that afternoon. They wanted to retire from city life, and as the man had explained, the description of the cottage seemed just right.

She felt a little strange selling the cottage. But did they have an option? What else could be done?

"It's exactly what we need," Mr. Greesh said, looking at his parents' contented faces. "And it is quite difficult to get a cottage in these parts. In fact, it would be good if we could find a slightly bigger one for ourselves. I need to be in the city only twice a week. The rest of the time, I'm travelling for business. I would really like to live out here in the country. Something about the size of this house you are living in, I would think," he added, looking around their living room.

Richard laughed. But then he was suddenly serious. Wasn't this what he really wanted? What he and Dorothy both wanted? They both knew they had to move to the city, to an area near the Kesslers, not necessarily a really religious one. But not yet. It was too soon. Even though they were becoming painfully aware that they no longer belonged in this village, no longer belonged in Protestant, Christian society, it was difficult to move. There was a certain security in the familiar.

Mr. Greesh was looking at him.

"We . . . we are thinking of selling, but I am not sure when," said Richard. "I will be in touch with you about it." Mr. Greesh looked delighted.

There is a loud sickening crash . . . blackness . . . a sound of tearing metal . . . incredible heat . . . the sound of dripping water . . . people screaming . . . flames . . . children crying . . .

Dorothy awoke with a start. It was the dream again, more vivid this time—incredibly, incredibly vivid. And it wasn't Southbroom.

ON A GOLDEN CHAIN

She got out of bed, only half awake. She could not bear to be dreaming this again. She had to get up and go into the kitchen to make some coffee.

Half asleep, she stumbled towards the kettle, filled it with water and went to plug it in. There was water everywhere, over the plug, the wires . . .

She didn't notice it. She was too sleepy. She plugged it into the wall. There was a flash . . . and then . . . blackness!

CHAPTER 16

Her head was aching. She felt strange. There was a pain in her arm. She was in bed, but it wasn't her own bed. This one was harder. Everything felt unfamiliar. Where was she? What was happening? Her head was aching terribly.

She slowly opened her eyes and saw Richard and Rabbi Kessler talking to a man with glasses whom she did not know. A man wearing a white coat.

None of them noticed that she had awakened, and she heard snatches of their conversation. The man, obviously a doctor, was talking about strain and shock, and the fact that if Richard had not had the electric circuitry properly grounded the results would have been much worse.

What had happened? She strained her mind

to remember, but she could remember nothing.

Rabbi Kessler noticed that she was awake.

"Hello, Esther," he said, coming over to her. "How are you feeling? You've had a nasty electric shock."

Esther? Esther? Why was he calling her Esther? And yet, the name Esther seemed to strike within her a very deep chord. It seemed to sound like her name. Where had Rabbi Kessler come up with it? Her favorite doll had been called Esther, and now Lucy's doll. But now it seemed very much like her own name. But how could it be?

"I'm, well, all right now, I suppose. Have I been talking in my sleep?" she asked. "What did I say?"

"Well," said the rabbi. "A lot of the time you were speaking in a language that sounded like Dutch. But it wasn't distinct, so I couldn't get many words out of it."

"Dutch," said Dorothy. "Does that mean that I come from Holland? I mean, Mr. Blackman did say there was a train crash in Holland. I must find out about it, I must. I must!"

She looked at Richard imploringly.

"Please let's go to Holland and find my parents."

"Dorothy, dear, please rest now. We're just so thankful that you're all right."

She felt herself becoming hot and cold all over, and the doctor intervened.

"Later," he said. "Later. I can't have her disturbed too much. She has been through a lot in the last two days."

Two days? Two days? What had happened?

"What happened to me?" she asked.

"You got a shock when you plugged in the kettle, fortunately cut short by your husband's rewiring of the house. You need rest, a lot of rest. I understand you have also been under a great deal of strain these last few months. Your husband has been telling me about it. But we will get you right."

"We will leave the house and move to the city," said Richard.

"Leave the house?" she asked, puzzled. "Already? Should we?"

Rabbi Kessler laughed. "You have been saying for the last two days that you want to leave the house and move."

"Oh," said Dorothy. "What else have I been saying?"

No one said anything.

"Please tell me," she said.

The doctor again intervened. "Perhaps tomorrow," he said.

"Where are the children?" asked Dorothy suddenly.

"Don't worry," said Rabbi Kessler. "They are at home with Sara Chanah."

"Are you managing?" she asked Richard.

"Well," he said, "I have been mostly with the Kesslers."

"You said that I said my name was Esther," she said. "That's a Jewish name, isn't it?"

"Very much so," said the rabbi.

"Then Esther I will be," she said.

An overpowering drowsiness came over her, and she shut her eyes.

For the next forty-eight hours, Dorothy felt herself going in and out of consciousness. Each time she would wake she would find either Richard, Rabbi Kessler or Sara Chanah at her bedside. She wondered what she had been saying to them, if she had spoken about her family, her Jewish family.

Once when she awoke she saw Rev. Purdy leaning over her and she heard herself screaming and screaming until he left, ushered out quickly but apologetically by the nurses. She wondered if she had said anything to him.

She was aware of a conference going on inside her head as though it had become a massive stadium with speakers on both sides. There would be arguments back and forth as to the merits and demerits of Judaism and Christianity. It was as if speakers, one at a time, would assume the platform and present their point of view, only to be refuted and contested by another.

Rabbi Kessler was at the conference and was one of the main speakers. Even Michael Kahn, the Reform rabbi and the Conservative rabbi, had quite a lot to add. Rev. Purdy often assumed the platform, and the previous minister, Rev. McLean, shouted about the dangers of hell-fire that awaited the "unsaved."

She felt exhausted by these debates. She felt that everything in her life, in her husband's and children's lives, depended on her decision as to who would win the debate.

Rev. Purdy spoke about the religion of love and freedom where there was no set of laws to be obeyed, where all a person had to do was believe. Love was everywhere. Then a group of people from Rev. Purdy's book on anti-Semitism, people in all different kinds of clothes, from periods of Jewish history, got up on the platform and showed their scars and wounds and burns to the perpetrators of this religion of love.

At one stage of the "conference," Rev. Purdy was banished, perhaps the time corresponding with his leaving the hospital ward. Some time later, the Reform and Conservative rabbis were banished, eventually leaving Rabbi Kessler and a few other Orthodox rabbis. With the banishment of the others, the atmosphere changed. There was still a debate, still an argument, but there were large books in front of them, probably the Talmud, and they were sitting and learning, discussing and deliberating, but the debate was different. At the center of these discussions and debates was a unity of eternal purpose and belief. Dorothy became calmer, and her condition improved.

ON A GOLDEN CHAIN

"What happened to me?" asked Dorothy, waking up three days later. "Why am I in the hospital? And where are the children?"

Again, Richard explained to her what had happened and told her that the children were at the Kesslers.

She breathed a sigh of relief.

"I am so glad," she said. "I am so glad they are with the Kesslers. I don't know what I would have done if you had sent them to stay with Rev. Purdy."

Richard shot her an odd glance but did not comment. He knew his wife had been mumbling strange, incomprehensible things, sometimes in English, at times in a strange Germanic language. And he knew he was not allowed to worry her.

Several times, she had dreamed about the train crash and her screams had echoed around the ward, but try as he might, he couldn't make out anything of what she was saying except that there was blood all over and the train had crashed.

She had referred to herself several times as Esther, at these times always using a childlike voice. At other times she was Dorothy or even Dorothea. Once she said in a clear voice, "I am Esther and you are Dorothy, but we look exactly alike, so who is who and who am I?"

At this point, Richard had resisted questioning her carefully. It was obviously confusion about her name. Dorothy had also shouted out that she was a Jew and that no one was going to change her.

There was one thing which she had said, however, that had caused both Richard and Rabbi Kessler, who was there at the time, a wave of excitement. She had once more assumed a childlike voice, a very upset childlike voice, and had spoken as if she was at a *Shabbos* table.

"Tatty! I've broken it! Your best crystal bottle, and I have grape juice all over my dress! Tatty, please don't make *Kiddush* yet—I've got to change. I was playing far away from the table, but my ball hit it." She began to whimper. "I'm sorry, Tatty."

Her speech once more became unintelligible.

"You see!" said Richard. "That proves she's Jewish. Just like the time she finished the *Shema* when we first met you. How did she know that?"

"Richard," said the rabbi. "I am also very excited about what she said, and I was when she finished the *Shema* at my house. But it didn't prove she is Jewish. Dorothy, I mean Esther, had done a lot of reading even before I met her. She has had a lot of contact with our family, and she has read many, many Jewish books. We don't know for *sure* where this is coming from."

They tried to question her, but to no avail. She just continued to mumble in her strange, Dutch-sounding language.

CHAPTER 17

Three weeks later, Dorothy, or rather Esther, as she occasionally liked being called, returned home, feeling somewhat shaky and weak from her experience. She also felt very confused, especially in her feelings about *Yiddishkeit*. In a way she felt she just didn't want to think about it. She would just wait for her mind to settle.

She could not relate to her expressed wish to leave their town. She did not feel ready to move into a religious area. At the same time, she knew that none of them truly belonged where they were. There was not one other person who would even remotely understand their conflicts. The people in their town just did not get excited about religion. They certainly would not let it interfere with or direct their lives. It was considered ill-mannered to talk too much about it. They had to move, both Richard and she knew that, but to have to live every day of one's life religious? They were just not ready for that.

As soon as she returned home, she went to the velvet-lined box and took out the star on the golden chain, the Jewish star. It was of red gold and must have been hand-made by a master goldsmith. The delicate but slightly uneven engraving around it gave testimony to that. She wondered for a long time if the engraving meant anything. She had meant to ask Rabbi Kessler but had never had a chance.

She wrapped it up and replaced it, closing the box with a snap. Were all these not signs enough that she was Jewish? Apparently not.

She heard the ring of the doorbell and wondered who it could be. Probably one of her friends. A fair number had come to visit her, bringing her all kinds of sweets and cakes which she was fast learning that she could not eat, a situation she was beginning to find very disconcerting. What does one do with a whole lot of food one can't actually eat? This more than anything else made her seriously consider moving very shortly.

She walked slowly to the door, feeling a little faint as she tended to at times. She opened it and then moved several steps back.

It was one of the women from the church, the head of the Women's Association, in fact. By the way she greeted Dorothy and the way she carried a large Bible, it was clear that this was an official visit. For a moment, Dorothy wanted to shut the door again, to say that she was feeling sick, that she was not allowed visitors.

Before Dorothy thought of anything, however, the woman walked through her entrance hall and seated herself in one of the chairs.

ON A GOLDEN CHAIN

Dorothy had no option but to sit opposite her.

"Dorothy," said the woman, in a silky voice which held a tone of underlying menace. "Dorothy, I have been hearing such strange things about you and your family. Rev. Purdy asked if I would come and see you. I hear you are all in the clutches of the devil and are in such confusion and spiritual darkness." A tear forced it's way out of one eye and started to trickle down her cheek. "We have been remembering you in prayer, dear Dorothy. We have been remembering you in prayer."

Dorothy shuddered. She wished someone would come and rescue her. She really didn't have the strength to confront this lady.

"When I heard about this awful shock you had, I thought at last that Divine punishment had come to claim you. And then you recovered, so you have been given another chance to return to the church. But don't push it too hard, dear Dorothy. Who knows what could happen to you next? And then you would be left in Eternal damnation. I had to come and see you to get you to repent and mend your ways."

Dorothy was still too flabbergasted to speak. Quite frankly, she couldn't think what she should say at this point. But the woman went on.

"I could not bear to think of you and your dear husband and your two innocent children burning in hell forever and ever," she said, trying to get across her point. Another tear rolled down her cheek.

How odd, thought Dorothy. Why did only one eye cry?

"I will pray for you," the woman said.

"No, no, please don't do that," said Dorothy.

The woman turned crimson and the veins stood out in her neck as she pronounced judgment.

"You have spurned the church and gone after an ancient,

antiquated religion which has never recognized the truth."

"I haven't said anything," said Dorothy quietly.

"Rev. Purdy and I are leaving you time to think about it," said the woman in a threatening voice. "We will give you another two months, after which time we will take quite drastic action to save your souls." She got up dramatically and left the house, leaving Dorothy wondering what she was going to do.

She was just making a cup of coffee when Richard returned home with the two children. She lost no time in telling him about the woman's visit.

"Two months," he muttered. "Plenty of time." He picked up the phone.

"Whom are you phoning?" she asked.

"Mr. Greesh," he said. "We must accept a buyer for our house while there is one. We will rent a house in the city, not too close to the Kesslers, and not in a religious area, but somewhere near to them, even in walking distance from them. No one will know us and we will sort ourselves out from there. We can decide where we really want to live. We can even buy a house in Rabbi Kessler's area once the money for the two houses comes through."

He dialed the Greeshes' number and spoke to them. They were delighted to hear the news. They would make arrangements as soon as possible.

"That decided things pretty quickly," said Dorothy laughing. Then she caught sight of her husband's face. He had the old, haunted, bitter look he had shown when he first told her how he had been teased for being Jewish.

"This is how it's been for Jews throughout history," he said, very sullenly. "Running from one place to another, belonging nowhere."

"Richard, don't think about it like that. We wanted to

move, didn't we? It just made the way clear for us. We can just leave here, never see anyone again."

"And my work?" he asked.

"Richard," she said. "How are you going to manage that?"

"It actually works out quite nicely with that," he said, his good humor reappearing. "I asked my manager last week if there was a chance of my getting a transfer to the city, and he said there should be no difficulty whatever. I can even carry over my leave with me. I have a lot of accumulated leave, and it would have been a pity to let go of it."

"I wonder when you'll do that?" said Dorothy. "Workaholics like you hardly ever take leave."

"I will, Dorothy, I will, but not for another seven months at least. Then, perhaps, we can continue our search."

Dorothy looked at him sharply. "Do you still want to do that?" she asked. "I thought we had given up a bit after Southbroom."

"Only temporarily," he said gaily. Now that they were going to leave their town, he felt as if a load had been taken off him.

Six weeks later the Wilson family moved, with no more forwarding address than a post office box number in the city, never to return to the town.

CHAPTER

18

Moving into the city was strange and quite different. Rabbi Kessler had tried to persuade them to move into his area, feeling that they needed a *frum* environment, but Richard very firmly refused. They had found a house for rent about ten blocks away from the rabbi. There, Richard felt they could enjoy the best of both worlds.

Despite Rabbi Kessler's pleas, they did not send the children to a Jewish school. Richard wanted them to have a firm foothold in the secular world with the best secular education. They would get their Jewishness from their home and from the contact with the Kesslers, which increased markedly as soon as they move in.

Richard started attending regular *shiurim* and he began to attend the morning *minyan* at the *shul*. Judaism was becoming meaningful for him, and he looked forward to his learning, especially with Rabbi Kessler.

The rabbi also put them in touch with the local *beis din*. Richard and Dorothy had a somewhat intense meeting with one of the rabbis. He was courteous but demanding in his questioning. They left feeling a little uncomfortable with an instruction to concentrate on learning and practicing Judaism.

Though they understood that this was necessary, both Dorothy and Richard felt a certain amount of pressure being placed upon them. They were somehow no longer absorbing Judaism at their own pace. It seemed they were being monitored in their observance by a Jewish court of law.

Richard had been subdued during the interview, and had in fact not mentioned the question of sports on *Shabbos*. He told Dorothy afterwards that he had felt at that point that he could not bring it up with the rabbi. As he got to know him better, he would explain it to him. In the meanwhile, Richard left his sports club in Bradford and did not contact another one.

The *beis din* also put pressure on them in the search for Dorothy's family and encouraged them to make definite plans for an overseas visit as soon as possible.

They were questioned carefully about the children's education, and though the rabbi of the *beis din* would have preferred that the children attend a Jewish school, he accepted the situation.

Lucy and Steven seemed to settle down fairly easily into their new school despite entering it in the middle of the school year. The children enjoyed the pleasant walk to school.

Over the few months following, life settled down to a daily routine. The Wilsons were becoming religious at a steady pace, which at times they felt was a little fast for them. They had a great deal of contact with the Kesslers and, in the beginning, had spent part of every *Shabbos* with them. They made other friends, too, both in the Jewish community and with some of the neighbors around them.

Richard took on the Hebrew name Reuven, which he had found out had been his grandfather's name. He hardly used the name, however. How could he possibly use it at work?

The transfer to the city as far as his work was concerned was a great success. He had come at the time most opportune for advancement, and the large branch had been delighted with his work. For the first time in his life, he was achieving true job satisfaction. He felt so confident that he actually began to wear a *yarmulka* to work, a real breakthrough.

They continued to keep in contact with the curator of the museum who had written to several places to gain as much information about the train crashes as possible.

Everything seemed to point to the one in Holland. This crash had occurred close to Amsterdam on the night train. The curator had managed to obtain several newspaper reports of the crash. The pictures, horrible, ghastly pictures, made Dorothy shudder when she looked at them. Pictures, however, somewhat different from Southbroom.

That Dorothy had been speaking a Dutch-sounding language also seemed to confirm that this was the one. They planned to go to Holland as soon as possible, to go through the papers themselves and to speak to the people as they had done in Southbroom.

The crash in Czechoslovakia fell away as they investigated it. It seemed to have been a military transport train. Various features made them scrap it from the list. This left, however, the crash in Dikbos, South Africa.

Neither Dorothy nor Richard would have considered it

very seriously, and they certainly would not have considered visiting there, had the date of the crash not been the second of April, Dorothy's supposed registered birthday.

The *beis din* was extremely excited about this and almost insisted that it be followed up, saying that if it was within the Wilson's means, they should include South Africa in their trip.

The will was almost settled. Dorothy had inherited a considerable amount of money. There had been legal complications due to her own status as a non-legally adopted daughter, but these had somehow been overcome. There was more than enough money to cover several such trips.

As time went on, definite arrangements were made for a trip for Richard and Dorothy to include Amsterdam, Johannesburg and Tel Aviv. The few days' stopover in Israel had been included so they could see and experience so many of the things and places they had been learning about.

It was decided that they would not include the children on the trip. They would stay with the Kesslers, an arrangement which caused the children a great deal of eager anticipation and excitement.

As the time drew near, Richard and Dorothy were also filled with excitement about the trip. They had originally not felt keen on visiting South Africa, but as they had read up on it, they had felt they would really enjoy it, a country of many different and interesting people and lifestyles. They had not realized that South Africa had such a thriving Jewish community or that it had large, modern cities even though Dikbos, the place of the train crash, was a small, somewhat isolated town where many of the trains did not stop over.

It was also a new experience for them, at least since they had had the children, to be going on holiday just by themselves, and even the anticipation of it made them see how

ON A GOLDEN CHAIN

beneficial to a relationship such a holiday could be.

They made a promise to one another that whatever they would find out or discuss or, in fact, not discover about Dorothy's family, they would enjoy discovering Holland, South Africa and Israel together.

The time for the trip arrived. Almost before they knew it, they were boarding the plane and waving goodbye to Lucy, Steven and the Kesslers.

CHAPTER

19

Dorothy could not help but feel a thrill of excitement as they landed at Schiphol Airport in Amsterdam. As the plane circled before coming down, she saw three large semi-circular canals sparkling in the early morning sunlight, giving the city a half-moon-like appearance.

"Beautiful, isn't it?" Richard said. "It's so exciting to go to a new place. I've never been here before."

"Neither have I," Dorothy began. "But actually, I might have been," she ended quietly.

They walked through the massive airport, stopping to look at the toy, perfume and souvenir shops. Richard left her outside a shop selling trinkets and went to change some travellers' checks. At the same time, he would arrange for a taxi to their hotel.

ON A GOLDEN CHAIN

"Which hotel are we going to?" she asked.

"I was told about several," he said. "I liked the sound of the Hotel Die Port van Cleve, and I reserved a place there. It's right in the center of the city, behind the Royal Palace, next to the post office. It's not a new hotel. It apparently has an atmosphere of older Amsterdam. The restaurants are separate, so we can organize our own food. We can get kosher food in various stores. And there is, apparently, a sandwich shop."

"Does that mean we only eat sandwiches?" Dorothy asked.

"No," Richard replied. "That sandwich shop is kosher, really kosher, and sells all kinds of things. You can eat there. We won't starve, I suppose."

They took a taxi and were soon speeding along the Amsterdam Hague Highway. The scenery was incredibly beautiful, far more beautiful than they had ever imagined.

They arrived at their hotel and were ushered up to their rooms. Dorothy had intended to start exploring the city straight away, but when she looked at the soft, luxurious looking beds, she found herself lying on one "just for a few minutes."

She awoke suddenly and looked around her. Richard was nowhere to be seen. She looked at her watch. She must have been asleep for at least three hours. She wondered what Richard had been doing.

She went to the window and looked out over the city. A city of canals it truly was! But she had never imagined that there were so many. They seemed to be taking the place of streets. Did people use boats instead of cars? She really had to see this!

She lay back on her bed, enjoying the comfort of the hotel room. Older hotel or not, it certainly was tastefully furnished, with an accent on comfort and convenience.

She dozed off again to be awakened by Richard unlocking the door, his arms filled with packages.

"You look as if you have just come back from a supermarket," she said, laughing.

"I have," he said. "I have tins and tins of tuna with a good *hechsher*, and *matzah* and soda, and all kinds of other things. Of course, I also bought plenty of paper cups and plates and plastic knives, forks and spoons."

"Did you explain to the hotel management that we have to picnic over here?" she asked.

"Oh yes," said Richard. "He quite understood. He said that quite often Jewish people stay in this hotel and either bring all their own things or else they eat at the sandwich shop."

"Where is the sandwich shop?" she asked. "Did you find out?"

"More or less," he said. "But the manager suggested that I speak to a Jewish shopkeeper down the road from the hotel. I went to the man. He was very pleased to see me, though a little uncomfortable about my *yarmulka*. I am not sure why. He surely must have seen a religious Jew before. Anyway, he is taking a few hours off for us tomorrow morning. He hands over the shop to his assistant for that time and he is going to take us around Amsterdam, around the Jewish places."

"And the sandwich shop?" she asked, as she opened a tin of tuna for them both.

"He gave me complete directions. All we need is a cab," he said. "In the meanwhile we will contact Mr. van Woekom, Mr. Blackman's contact. He is expecting us. He seems to know quite a bit of English, thank goodness. Apparently we are to go through some of the papers with him."

No sooner said than done. They put through the call to

Mr. van Woekom, a charming man who spoke English well, with a heavy Dutch accent.

He said he was expecting them, and if they felt they had recovered sufficiently from their trip, he would meet them at three p.m. at the railway offices. He gave them the exact directions.

"That gives us time to phone the Kesslers to see how the children are and then to find our sandwich shop," said Richard. "At least, we have somewhere we can eat."

"What would happen if we were in a place where there wasn't anything kosher?" asked Dorothy.

"I'm not sure," said Richard. "Rabbi Kessler said we should take food with us when we travel. But I wonder what would happen if we just went into a restaurant and ate only fish. I mean, who would complain?"

"We aren't supposed to do that," said Dorothy.

"I mean," said Richard, "who would know?"

"Hashem would," said Dorothy. "That's why we are keeping kosher in the first place."

Richard kept quiet. Such a statement seemed to have no real answer.

"I've got the directions," he said. "I'll call a cab."

As they saw the row of shops pointed out by the cab driver, Richard could not help smiling as he saw one had a Coca Cola sign, a Hebrew "kosher" sign and, written in English, "Sol's Sandwich Shop."

A delicious aroma of meat and fresh bread greeted them as they reached the door of the tiny shop. They were delighted to find that they could buy anything *fleishig*, from meatballs and brisket to cold meats. This certainly beat tuna!

As she looked around, Dorothy noticed a trophy about one and a half feet tall. "A skater?" she asked no one in particular.

ON A GOLDEN CHAIN

A tall man with a *yarmulka* who was sitting and eating when they came in, answered. "That trophy is very much prized in Holland," he said, "and Sol got it. For that he had to complete a twenty city race in good time. He had to skate on all the frozen rivers and lakes. We don't have the race often, because it's rare for all the cities to ice up together. Four years ago, however, there it was again. And we are very proud of our Sol."

Sol, who stood behind the counter preparing food, gave a slow smile. He had trained hard and long for that trophy, and he was justly proud of it.

Richard and Dorothy ate hungrily. They had not realized how hungry they were.

"I think you had better stock up with food in your hotel," the tall man suggested. He directed them to a shop ten minutes walk away.

The Wilsons were delighted to find that they could buy all kinds of foods with a reliable *hechsher*. There was also a bakery which sometimes sold Jewish bread, and of course, there was the bakery run by Sol's father. Things were definitely looking up.

At exactly two-fifty, Richard and Dorothy arrived at the station offices. Mr. van Woekom was as charming in person as he had been on the telephone.

"Sit down, sit down," he said to them, ushering them into a comfortably furnished office.

Mr. Blackman had been very thorough in his search. Mr. van Woekom knew their whole story very well. He had made his own plans for their research on the crash. First, he gave the exact directions as to the location of the crash, just outside Amsterdam. They would obviously want to visit it. He then suggested that perhaps they could actually take a trip on the NS night train, using the same route to see if in that way,

ON A GOLDEN CHAIN

memories could be awakened. He did not notice that Dorothy had whitened and that her hands had started to shake a little. He said he had been in contact with the main newspaper offices several times, and that Mr. van Aarent was expecting them either that day or the following one. He gave them the names of several people who had been involved in the crash, people who would remember something. One of these people, a Mr. Grunberg, was a religious Jew. He and his wife had both been on the train at the time of the crash. He then looked at his watch. "Mr. Geerling will be here in about ten minutes," he said. "He remembers the crash very well. Unfortunately, he speaks very little English, but I will translate for you."

They waited for him, declining Mr. van Woekom's offer of tea and cake. He was not surprised. He had met Jews before, even religious ones.

There was a knock at the door, and Mr. Geerling entered. He looked nervously at Richard and Dorothy and sat opposite them, tapping his feet rhythmically on the ground. Dorothy wished she could tell him to stop doing this. Why was he so nervous?

Mr. van Woekom spoke to Mr. Geerling almost as one would speak to a child, comforting him and encouraging him. He told them about the crash, described it in graphic detail. As he got into the story, his head of white hair seemed to shake in unison with the tapping of his feet. He looked distressed, but at the same time, detached.

The crash had not been as catastrophic as that of Southbroom, but several people had been killed and many injured.

"Please ask him if anyone was missing, if a child was missing," said Dorothy.

The man's eyes started to bulge when Mr. Von Woekom

117

translated Dorothy's question. Sweat stood out on his forehead.

"I don't know," Mr. Geerling replied. "Maybe, but I didn't hear. I don't know. I don't remember."

Dorothy had been wondering what was wrong with Mr. Geerling. She realized he was suffering from fear and shock. Had this been as a result of the accident? An accident of twenty-three years ago?

When he finished his story and there were no more questions, he left the room, a quivering mass of what seemed like involuntary movements.

"He has been like this since the crash," Mr. van Woekom explained. "Sometimes even for weeks at a time, he is a little better, and then he works for us in the office, doing only light work. But if you speak to the older people here, they will tell you that since the crash he has only been partly himself. The other half was one of the casualties."

Both Richard and Dorothy were deeply affected by the man's fear and anxiety. They remembered the railway workers in Southbroom who had been affected by it. A train crash carried a terrible toll, not only in the obvious victims. Dorothy was not one of the obvious victims. In fact, had anyone really looked for her?

They left Mr. van Woekom's office with a promise to keep him informed of their progress, and they went back to their hotel.

As they passed one of the hotel restaurants, Richard was suddenly bowled over by the smell of roasted meat and hot sausages.

"I wish I weren't Jewish," he said to Dorothy. "I wish I could be not Jewish or not religious or whatever, just for an hour. Just enough time to have dinner in that restaurant. I would start with mouth-watering soles and lobsters, followed by mushroom soup and then I would have roast leg of lamb."

"Richard, stop that," said Dorothy. "We bought a lot of food from Sol's shop and from the other one. We'll have a good meal upstairs."

"But it will be cold," said Richard, pretending to enter the restaurant door. Dorothy ran towards him and he laughed.

"Don't worry," he said. "I am only teasing you. We will enjoy our meal upstairs. I am sure we will. After we eat, we will go to the newspaper offices. They are apparently open twenty-four hours a day, and the man who knows about us is on an afternoon-early evening shift, off at ten p.m."

"That will be enough for one day. We only arrived this morning," said Dorothy. "We'll put it all together tomorrow."

The man in the newspaper office to whom they had been referred looked incredibly pleased to see them. They would conduct their own research!

He soon realized, however, that their knowledge of the language was fairly minimal and that they needed his translation abilities to help them.

He brought out the huge, bound volumes which showed the dramatic pictures of the accident which the Wilsons had already seen, and was soon explaining all that was depicted.

"Please read me the names of the people who were killed and injured," said Dorothy.

"Well, there were so many injured that they didn't list them, but the dead . . ." He read out the names and ages slowly, steadily, names which even twenty-three years later gave a sense of the tragedy involved. There was no record of any adult or child missing.

Dorothy was holding her breath. She had hoped to hear, and at the same time dreaded hearing, a name which would strike some chord of memory. She felt relieved that none had done so. She had not wanted her family to be among the dead.

They spent at least two hours looking though the large bound volumes. "I think we should go back," Dorothy said. "I can't stay here any longer. I am beginning to cough from the dust. Twenty-three years of dust."

They blinked as they emerged from the dark newspaper office into the city. Amsterdam at night. Tomorrow, they would explore it more thoroughly.

CHAPTER 20

"To which *shul* are you taking us to?" Dorothy asked the old man who was taking them for a tour of Jewish Amsterdam.

"Let me explain," he said. "Many of us don't actually *belong* to a *shul*. It isn't that we don't want to identify as Jews. We are very proud to be Jews. But we don't want our names on lists."

He shuddered. Dorothy was reminded that caution and even fear still stalked the Jewish community in Holland. Almost fifty years ago they had been hunted through their membership lists, and they would not allow such lists to exist again!

"But I can show you some interesting *shuls*." He looked at Richard's *yarmulka*. "You would like the Kollel Shul."

He told them about the two main *shuls* in

Amsterdam, one of which was the seat of the Rabbi President.

"You mean the chief rabbi?" Dorothy asked.

"No, Rabbi President," said the man. "There are four chief rabbis, but the Rabbi President is the Rabbi President. You'll find the *shul* near the Apollo Hotel."

"Are the *shuls* very old?" asked Richard.

"No," said the man. "Actually, they are not. Only one *shul* survived the war. Two, actually, but everything else was destroyed."

"How did they survive?" asked Dorothy.

"One *shul* was disguised," he said. "It's still a *shul* until this day. But it was on an upper floor of a building, and people managed to disguise it as a warehouse during the war. The Germans never found it."

"That's strange," she said. "It's odd to have a *shul* on an upper story of a building. Usually, a *shul* is in a building of its own."

"Not really," he said. "The Kollel Shul is on the ground floor of a building. Nothing strange about that. You'll feel very much at home there. There are many English-speaking, *frum* men learning there," he said. "I am also going to take you to the old Portuguese *shul*. It isn't always open to visitors, but I can take you there. It was saved during the war, because it enjoyed some kind of special rights of the Portuguese Embassy."

They arrived at the building which was surrounded by walls so massive that there were offices and various rooms constructed within them. They went through the thick gateway. This was certainly a fortified building.

"This was built by the *marranos*," said the man. "Built by the *marranos* who came from Spain and Portugal to Holland, land of religious tolerance."

Dorothy looked at the beautiful old *shul* which was

apparently hardly used. Even the regular *minyan davened* in one of the side rooms, rather than in the main *shul*. Several of the window panes were broken. Dorothy rubbed her hand along one of the carved wooden benches. So many things here seemed to be made of wood.

Twelve solid pillars supported the women's section. Dorothy and Richard were both impressed with the many massive candelabra. As there was no electricity, these remained as they had been for centuries.

"They say there are six hundred and thirteen of them," the man was saying. "They are symbolic, I have heard, of the six hundred and thirteen laws Jews used to keep."

Dorothy shuddered. Here they were in a *shul* which echoed Jewish history from every side. Yet, to many people in the city which apparently had had such a vibrant and thriving community, Jewish laws were merely a part of their historic past.

She quietly walked over to the wooden *chuppah* on the side of the *shul*, its carved ceiling held up by solid pillars. How many weddings had been held here?

For a few moments, she tried to go back in time, to envision the Spanish and Portuguese Jews, safe in Holland, safe in this fortress of a *shul*, safe to conduct their weddings without fear of the Inquisition.

She knew that many of them had had to pretend to practice certain Catholic rituals, and she wondered if *their* children had ever become confused.

The man was showing Richard the old *aron kodesh*, ornately and beautifully carved. Again they noted the bad state of disrepair of the *shul*. Dorothy wanted to cry out that Judaism was alive and would never die.

A strange feeling of heaviness overcame her, and feelings of despair churned within her. Would she ever find her family? Wasn't she just chasing a dream? Would she spend her life going from city to city looking for them?

She was still feeling unhappy when she came out of the fortress-like walls and heard the noise of the people in the nearby flea market. The man pointed out to them the statue of the Dock Worker.

Dorothy was feeling incredibly tired. The strain was taking it's toll. She should rest. She knew she should rest. Richard gave her a concerned glance.

"We had better go back," he said. "Would you like to come with us to the sandwich shop?" he asked the man.

"I would love to, but I have to be back at my work. I will leave you there and perhaps we can meet again."

Richard thanked him, knowing that without him they would never have seen the truly Jewish side of Amsterdam.

Richard had arranged with several of the people on the list to visit them that afternoon. When Dorothy saw the appointment list in his hand, marked by the hours, she laughed, saying it made him look like an insurance salesman or a dentist. She realized that Richard had no intention of making this a relaxing trip. They had come with a purpose, and that purpose had to be fulfilled.

They were fortunate that most of the people they had arranged to see could speak at least some English. They communicated fairly well with many of them. They learned a great deal about the crash, but nothing of any real significance to Dorothy.

The Grunberg family was the last appointment on the list. They felt that a Jewish family would know more clearly which Jews were involved in the crash. They also felt they would like to talk to them, perhaps to get to know them a little. They missed their contact with religious Jews.

They arrived at the seventeenth-century house and noted

the *mezuzah* on the door. This was definitely the right place. Richard rang the bell and waited. There was a shuffling behind the door and a bearded man with a *yarmulka* opened it.

"Mr. Wilson," he said rather formally.

When he noticed Richard's *yarmulka*, his demeanor changed. "Please come in," he said warmly. "You wanted to speak to us." He ushered them into the living room, asking his wife to make them some coffee.

Dorothy was soon telling her entire story to both of them. Mrs. Bella Grunberg seemed very moved by it.

"I don't know if we can help you," she said. "I never heard about a missing child. But we want to help you all we can. We must see one another again. I will speak to people for you, people who might know."

"It is Wednesday already," said Mr. Grunberg. "It is very difficult to spend *Shabbos* in a hotel, even though Sol sells food for *Shabbos* which even tastes good cold. But please come to us. Meanwhile, we will try to find out as much as we can. We would love to have you. Please be here at around five-thirty p.m. on Friday. Someone will take you back to your hotel after *Shabbos*."

Both Dorothy and Richard felt very relieved not to have to spend *Shabbos* in the hotel, and they agreed readily. That was something really to look forward to, and by that time they should be quite far ahead in their search.

They returned to their hotel, once more unpacking the food they had bought from Sol and his father. Dorothy tried to arrange it as aesthetically as possible and eventually put most of it away in the cupboard. She looked doubtfully at her handiwork.

"I think we are making a bit of a mess over here," she said.

"Don't worry," he said. "We are paying enough for the

room. They will clean it up afterwards."

She was beginning to feel tired, but she realized that Richard had every intention of going out.

"We are going to explore the city," he announced. "I have been reading the tourist handbooks. This is a city of canals, and we are going on a boat. To really see Amsterdam, my book says, we have to see it from the canals."

An hour later they were sitting in a tubular, glass-covered boat which sat low in the water, making other boats tower above them. They realized, now, why Amsterdam was called the City of Canals. A whole set of bridges stretched out in front of them, a sight which Dorothy felt she would never forget.

As they turned into the Prinsengracht, someone pointed out the apartment where Anne Frank and her family had hidden. Dorothy and Richard felt a heavy sadness as the shadow of the war fell over them. But hadn't they seen it before in the eyes and actions of the Jews of Holland? They had seen the way they would not let themselves be listed as synagogue members. It was apparent in the way they related to Richard's *yarmulka*.

"Amsterdam has a hundred sixty-five canals and over a thousand bridges," the tour guide was saying.

They looked once more at the water surrounding them and at the line of bridges in front of them. People were riding or pushing bicycles across the bridges. They could see why Amsterdam was also referred to as "a city of bicycles."

The houses on either side of them spoke of the majestic beauty of seventeenth-century Amsterdam. Some, admittedly, were in great need of repair, but their past grandeur was not entirely lost. Others had been turned into factories and warehouses.

Some two hours later, they left the boat and looked

around the shops. They walked into the greater part of the town, to the end of a street and looked at the canal. It looked so strange—a street leading to a watery roadway.

Dorothy looked at the old buildings around her, feeling a strange sensation of the familiar. Could she have known this street? But there were many such streets in Holland, each leading to a river. Was it this one? Even the smell seemed familiar. She stood, looking into the water, and as she saw her face reflected back she started feeling faint and giddy. Was that her reflection? She stared at the water as if hypnotized.

Richard watched her, not quite sure whether to interrupt her thoughts. Perhaps this was important. Maybe one of the many missing pieces of the jigsaw would fit in somewhere. His wife was obviously remembering something.

Almost as if feeling his stare, she looked around. "Richard," she said. "Richard, I am sure I have been here before. This part seems so familiar." She looked around her, trying at the same time to reach into the recesses of her mind to connect with something. "Or was it . . . was it just looking at my reflection in the water? Staring at the image of myself?"

She looked back into the water, and the world seemed strangely quiet in spite of the not too distant crowds and the peddler proclaiming his wares.

They continued to explore the city, the museums and the art galleries. Midnight found them looking over the Skinny Bridge on the River Amstel. It was breathtakingly beautiful. The water seemed at this hour to reflect centuries upon centuries.

Richard looked at her. "Are you sleepy?" he asked.

"No, no, not at all," she said. "I am wide, wide awake."

"What do you think of taking Mr. van Woekom's suggestion and taking the NS night train? It runs every hour from one a.m."

Dorothy felt her heart stand still and her hands begin to shake. But she knew she had to go. "Where does it go, exactly?" she asked.

"Amsterdam, Schiphol Airport, the Hague, Rotterdam," he said. "The crash was just outside Amsterdam, but we will see the place tomorrow. We can't see much at night."

"Why do you want to go on the night train?" she asked.

"All right," he said. "I am sorry. It is a crazy idea. We'll do it in the daytime. I suppose we should go back to the hotel now."

"No," she said, trying to sound lighthearted. "I would love to go."

They made their way to the station and booked two round-trip tickets. It was not long before the sleek, yellow train arrived and they climbed onto it.

It was only when they were quite far out of the station that Richard noticed that Dorothy was shaking. Her face, even her lips, had become very pale.

"You are tired," he said in a worried tone. "Or are you sick?"

"No, no, I am not tired or sick," she stammered. "It was important, very important to go on a train, on this train."

Richard stared at her, and his eyes became wide as he realized what was happening. "This is the first time," he said. "I should have known. We have never been on a train together. You have never been on a train since . . ." He paused.

"Since the accident," she completed the sentence for him.

"I'm sorry," he said. "I didn't realize." He looked around at the almost empty train compartment.

"Don't be sorry, Richard. I did this on purpose. I thought . . . I thought I might remember something," she said.

"Do you?" asked Richard. "Do you remember anything?"

ON A GOLDEN CHAIN

She laughed. "Richard, we only just got onto the train."

"But you do," he insisted. "Otherwise, why are you shaking like that?"

"Something inside me remembers, but not me, as yet." She looked outside the window at the light flashing past. She was becoming very sleepy. It was, after all, one-thirty a.m.

She awoke to the sound of screaming.

Who was screaming like that? And why were Richard and the other passengers in the compartment bending over her? Why didn't they attend to the person who was screaming? It took her at least a minute to realize that she was the one screaming, and she sat up, feeling embarrassed.

"I'm sorry," she said, and then she whispered, "The train crash. It was in the early morning, long, long before the sun came up. It was dark, and everyone was screaming, screaming!"

CHAPTER 21

The next morning, Dorothy woke up late, her head pounding. She felt ill, sore and frightened. Her whole body would not stop trembling. Had she become like Mr. Geerling? And where was Richard? Had he gone out? When would he be back? And what were they going to do today?

When she remembered that they had planned to go to the scene of the crash, she felt more ill. She had to do these things, she knew she had to do these things, but it was taking an extremely hard toll on her emotional and physical state.

Richard, somehow realizing she was awake, tiptoed into the room. "Dorothy," he said. "I'm sorry. I can't tell you how sorry I am. I should never have taken you on a train again. We must forget this whole thing. It's just too much for you."

ON A GOLDEN CHAIN

For some reason, Richard's reaction seemed to settle Dorothy and she felt her old strength return. She sat up.

"Richard, I knew it would be hard. But that is why we are here. I have to know who I am. We have to find my family, and I feel we're getting closer. This must be the right train crash."

"But there are no little girls missing," said Richard. "I phoned all the other people on the list and spoke to them. They didn't come up with much. I think that is why they were near the end of the list."

"We must carry on," said Dorothy. "We must go to the crash site straight away. Please! Let's go while I can still take it. I'll eat something quickly, some of that apple strudel, and then we should go. You can call a taxi in forty-five minutes. I will be dressed and ready."

True to her word, Dorothy was ready on time, and the taxi sped with them to the site of the crash, just outside Amsterdam. She did not remember it from the night before. How could she have? She was asleep, or screaming the compartment down, or both.

They asked the taxi to wait with them. They had no intention of boarding another train in Holland. They seemed to arrive quite suddenly at a part of the railway line lined with trees and surrounded by masses of yellow flowers. Was this the scene of the crash? Nothing seemed familiar, but then, years had gone past, and she had been a child. How could it seem familiar?

She looked up at the trees towering above her. Was this the forest? It couldn't be, because there were scarcely three rows lining the railway lines. She looked around. There was no forest, but then, anything could have happened in the last twenty-three years. Forests did get chopped down.

She shuddered as she heard a train approaching. It looked quite beautiful and majestic with its yellow color matching the flowers around it and yet, to her, it was an instrument of terror. She stiffened, hardly breathing until it had gone past. Then she turned to Richard.

"I think perhaps it isn't this crash," she said slowly, in an almost childish voice. "It's somewhere else." He could see that she was on the verge of tears.

"Let's forget about it now," he said. "We'll discuss it later. I'm hungry."

He directed the driver to Sol's Sandwich Shop and leaned back. He too was tired, overwhelmingly tired, and he felt an odd disappointment, even an anger that his wife had not recognized the place. Was there a train crash?

It had to be in Holland. What about that strange Dutch-sounding language she had spoken after the shock? Was there really another family? Maybe Nana had become confused before she had died. But there had been a star, a star on a golden chain, the star Dorothy had worn around her neck. That was real.

They arrived at Sol's, ordered food and ate heartily. Other regular visitors to Sol's had begun to recognize them, and they found themselves surrounded by friendly faces inquiring about how they were enjoying their trip. Richard enjoyed the sense of camaraderie.

They wandered around the souvenir shops, selecting presents to take back home. "Let's look at the newspapers again," said Dorothy. "Maybe there is something. Maybe there is something about a missing child."

They made their way back to the offices, pleased to see that the man to whom they had originally spoken was on duty. He sent them downstairs. They knew where to go. They told him they might be two or three hours.

There was silence in the archives of the newspaper offices. Silence, except for the rustle of papers in the twenty-year-old heavy bound volumes. They had been looking for hours. The man who worked there was not with them. He was busy in the office above.

"I will come if you need something translated," he had said. "If they were looking for you, there would be a picture."

Looking for a picture, they searched as far as two years after the accident, but they found nothing relevant.

"Shall we stop or carry on?" asked Dorothy.

"Let's just take one more year," said Richard. "We are here in Amsterdam. We will never have this opportunity again." And he pulled out another volume.

It took them another hour to look through it. Dorothy turned to him.

"I think we have the wrong crash again," she said. "Or maybe I just remember everything wrong. Maybe it was even Southbroom. I think we should see what the Grunbergs say. If they come up with nothing, we'll leave on Monday, or even Sunday."

"The plane to Johannesburg leaves on Monday," said Richard.

"Maybe we should just book provisionally for that flight. I must see Dikbos. That is the only other place. We have to go there as soon as possible."

They arrived at the Grunberg residence at exactly five-thirty.

Mr. and Mrs. Grunberg were overwhelming in their welcome. They ushered Richard and Dorothy into a large, comfortable bedroom with a bathroom and small lounge leading off from it. Everything in the home was expensively but tastefully furnished.

"As we told your husband, Dorothy, my dear," Mrs. Grunberg said, "everything here is absolutely, one hundred percent kosher. It's been difficult over the last few years. Sometimes, we had to go without quite basic things, but we have always managed."

Mr. Grunberg called his wife away, saying that they would all speak over the *Shabbos* table. In the meanwhile, candle-lighting was barely twenty-five minutes away.

Mr. Grunberg made *Kiddush*. They washed and ate *challah*. Mrs. Grunberg served the fish, and now was the time to talk.

"I can't wait," said Bella Grunberg. "I just have to know. How, when you were lost as a child, how did you know you were Jewish? How did you remain *frum*?"

Dorothy smiled. "That's a very long story," she said.

"We have time," said Mr. Grunberg. "We have time. We have a whole *Shabbos*."

Dorothy once more told her story, this time including the Kesslers and her searching, Richard filling in when she seemed at a loss for words. Both Mrs. and Mrs. Grunberg could not take their eyes off of them as they hung on to every word.

"We are starving our guests, Bella," her husband said, standing up. "We had better get them some soup. We won't let them talk until after they've eaten," he added, laughing.

"Don't think this is all to be without reward," said Richard. "It will be your turn soon."

However, it was at least two hours later before the Grunbergs made their contribution. They had both been very involved in everything Dorothy and Richard had to say. The two young people before them had an amazing story. They were afraid, however, that they were going to disappoint them.

Mr. Grunberg turned to them. "Hashem has led you this far. I am sure you will be led to reunite with your family."

ON A GOLDEN CHAIN

Dorothy suddenly felt ashamed. There were times when she had almost forgotten this. There were times that she had allowed feelings of desolation to creep into her soul and blot out her awareness that Hashem runs the world. There were times when she had felt desperately alone, even with Richard. Mr. Grunberg's words at the *Shabbos* table put things back into perspective.

It wasn't that she and Richard were two isolated human beings searching for figures from her past. She and Richard had been drawn out of the depths of assimilation and planted firmly in the orchards of *Yiddishkeit*. She would trust Hashem in the same way to lead her to her family, whether it was this week, this month, or even this decade. She would do her part and search for them. But she would never again give way to despair. She had had so much faith and trust, but she had somehow let it slip.

It was thus, when Mr. Grunberg told her that they had no real news for her, that she did not despair. She looked into the flames of the *Shabbos* candles which had burned to a quarter of their size, and she truly felt the peace of *Shabbos*.

CHAPTER 22

"We will be landing in Johannesburg in five minutes. Fasten your seat belts."

Dorothy listened to the announcements. She was beginning to know them by heart. She was sure she could give a public demonstration of how to use the life-jackets and the oxygen masks.

The announcer switched to another language. Strange, why should he make the announcements in Dutch again? He had stopped doing this as he left Amsterdam. She mentioned her puzzlement to Richard. The man sitting in front of them overheard her.

"That isn't Dutch, madam," he said, "It is a very similar language called Afrikaans. In South Africa people speak both English and Afrikaans."

Dorothy felt herself go cold. It wasn't the news that the Dutch-sounding language could be

Afrikaans, it was the man's accent. She had heard that accent before, never having realized it was an accent. The man spoke exactly like her adoptive father!

But there was no time for thinking. The plane was circling the airport. They would soon be there.

It was not until they were in a taxi on the way to the Connoisseur Hotel that Dorothy was able to speak to Richard about her father's accent. By that time she had heard it spoken by many people—the customs officials, the bank tellers as they had changed some of their travellers' checks, and fellow passengers.

As soon as she mentioned it, Richard exclaimed, "That's it! The way Nana spoke. I knew the accent reminded me of something. I knew I had heard it before."

"It reminds me more of the way my father spoke," said Dorothy.

"Do you know what that means?" said Richard. "I have been listening to the language. It is very much like Dutch or Hollands as they call it. This means that your parents probably came from South Africa."

"And therefore," said Dorothy, "this is probably the right train crash. At last!"

"At last," said Richard. "But it just had to be because this is the only one left, as far as I know, anyway."

They were delighted to find that the Connoisseur Hotel was on a par with some of the best hotels. Neither of them had been to a kosher hotel of that standard before, nor had they really known that such hotels existed in the Jewish world.

When they phoned the Kesslers that evening to speak to the children, Rabbi Kessler laughed at their surprise. "You haven't yet travelled the Jewish world," he said. "Only Amsterdam, and that didn't have a kosher hotel at all."

A pity, thought Richard, that they were to be in

ON A GOLDEN CHAIN

Johannesburg for only one or two days, until they made final arrangements for their trip to Dikbos.

It was, in fact, three days later that Richard and Dorothy, armed with map book, directions and a supply of non-perishable kosher food, started on their journey to Dikbos in their small rented Avis Mazda 323.

They were aware that there was a drive of hundreds of kilometers in front of them. They would be driving south, over the Vaal River into the Orange Free State. They were going to break their journey somewhere in the Free State for an overnight stop.

They had enjoyed being in Johannesburg, enjoyed meeting people from so many different groups and cultures. They had even done a bit of touring and had been down a disused mine, open to tourists.

They had been warned that the scenery they would pass would be at times incredibly, breathtakingly beautiful, and at other times flat, monotonous and boring. In fact, as they finally neared Dikbos, Dorothy had to keep talking to Richard to stop him from falling asleep at the wheel.

As they drew closer to the border, however, they found that the scenery once more changed. There were now many hills and forests. Once again they were both inspired by the beauty of the scene around them. There were no hotels in Dikbos, only a small guest home run by a Mrs. van Rensberg.

Richard had called her from Johannesburg, and she had welcomed their intended visit to her home. She had been somewhat suspicious, however, that they would not eat her food. It had taken long explanations about Jews and Judaism, and what they had to do with food. Eventually he had somehow made it clear that he would be quite prepared to pay full board and lodging, and still reluctantly, she had agreed, muttering something about these strange diet fads.

Dikbos was a small town, almost a village, nestled at the foot of the mountains. On its right was a fairly small but dense forest, which to a child could have seemed endlessly large and frightening.

There was a modest station, quaintly built, which looked completely innocent of being the scene of a major accident so many years before. Close to it was a lake, its waters green and sparkling in the sunlight. In fact, the town looked as if it hadn't awakened for years.

The guest house, built in the Cape Dutch style, was homey and comfortable. Despite the dreadful memories, which Dorothy could hardly equate with this peaceful, gentle place, Dorothy felt happy at the thought of spending time in such beautiful surroundings. This town could have been the home of her parents, her adoptive parents.

Perhaps in some way she could find out more about them, though of course they might have changed their last name—very probably they had. She would make that search also, because she had really loved them.

Richard thought that the owners of the guest house might tell them something about the train crash, but though they obviously remembered it, it was something they preferred not to discuss. In fact, Richard soon realized, there was a certain studied silence when he questioned anyone around the town. He was also aware that, where people in Johannesburg he had met spoke mostly English, the people here tended to be predominantly Afrikaans-speaking, although they understood English fairly well and could communicate in English.

The station master, obviously too young to remember the crash, was more helpful. He produced a small booklet about the railways in which the ghastly details were given, most of which the Wilsons had heard before. One hundred ninety people dead, sixty injured and twenty-eight missing, believed drowned.

They had never read before about the drowning. Was the lake so near to the station? Richard asked the station master about this.

"I have heard," he said, "that the coaches came right off the rails very close to the lake. People could easily have been thrown into it. The accident was caused by a massive tree blocking the lines, which was out of sight of the driver in the pre-dawn light. Apparently the tree had been uprooted during a flash thunderstorm, which can be so dangerous at times."

Seeing that the man truly had no more information, the Wilsons looked once again at the site of the crash. They were still looking when the man beckoned them to come to the other side of the line, the lake side. Dorothy gasped.

"This is it," she said, panting. "I was lying here and I was looking at myself." She realized that the station master was looking at her oddly and she went on. "I mean, I must have been lying there, and then I somehow got up and saw everyone lying there."

They went back to the guest home and ate some of the rolls and grilled chicken which they had brought with them from the Connoisseur Hotel, being somewhat apprehensive of the days when they would have to start eating *matzah*, pickled cucumbers and tuna. They had noticed, as they passed the dining room, how everyone was eating thick slices of freshly baked bread with butter churned only that morning, together with all kinds of things which made their mouths water despite themselves.

Tomorrow, Mrs. van Rensberg said, they were going to roast a lamb on the spit—a pity they could not join them.

ON A GOLDEN CHAIN

Surely, an exception could be made just this once?

After resting for an hour, they set out towards the forest. Mrs. van Rensberg warned them that it was easy to get lost there and that it was thicker and more confusing than they thought. She spoke darkly about people who had gone there and never come out again. But, she explained further, in her strongly accented, limited English, there was a path, and if they followed it and stuck to it, they should be safe.

With her careful directions they found the path almost immediately and set off along it. They had not gone very far when Dorothy started to have sudden overwhelming feelings of anxiety.

"All the trees, the trees just covering you," she said. "It just makes me feel so nervous. They are so tall, so frightening."

Richard had been finding the forest incredibly beautiful, but he understood his wife's anxiety. "Do you want to leave?" he asked.

"Of course not," she said. "This is why we are here, isn't it? To find out where I come from, about my past."

They walked on. There was silence except for the crackling of dead leaves under their feet. It *was* beautiful, truly beautiful. The sun shone through the trees, making radiant patterns on the leaves and on the ground. Everything smelled so fresh.

"One could get lost here," said Dorothy suddenly. "Mrs. van Rensberg said so."

"Don't worry," said Richard. "I know where I am going. I am keeping my position from the position of the sun. It is still possible to see it through the trees. You can see it even more clearly in some ways, because you can see where it is shining."

They could hear the sounds of small animals and birds, but they themselves again became silent, just walking.

ON A GOLDEN CHAIN

Suddenly, they came upon a cottage in the forest. It had probably once been a very spacious, lovely cottage, but now the windows were broken and shattered. No one could possibly be living there. Could this have been her parents' home? Dorothy searched and searched her mind, but she could remember nothing.

They walked up to the door which was still in fairly good condition and tried it. It opened quite easily, without even a squeak. Could someone be living there? It had a strange atmosphere of both being lived in and deserted, and yet neither Dorothy nor Richard really took the idea of their being intruders seriously.

Everything looked as if it had not been touched for years. The cottage was fairly well built, and though left to time and the elements, it was still very strong.

It was filled with dusty, aging furniture. There was a bedroom with two beds and a smaller, home-made one where a child could have slept. There was a cupboard with only one door and a chest of drawers which had been broken and therefore would not close properly.

The living room-dining room area contained chairs whose stuffing was removed, and on one of the chairs, to Dorothy's disbelief, was a purring, well-fed black cat, a domestic cat, obviously someone's pet. But what was he doing here?

For the first time, they really considered the possibility of someone living there. Too late, however. They were suddenly greeted with screams and strange cackling laughter.

A witch, thought Dorothy, her anxiety returning. But how could this be in this day and age? Richard later asserted that his first impression of the woman had also been that she was a witch, especially as she was waving a stick at them, shouting in some strange language, only part of it sounding like Afrikaans. She appeared deaf to any of their apologies and literally drove them out of the house and back along the forest path.

They returned to their small guest home looking quite flustered. As soon as she looked at them, Mrs. van Rensberg realized what had happened and explained to them about the strange, harmless woman inhabiting the forest.

The woman was "old Kerry," said to be a gypsy and sometimes said to be a witch, but probably neither of these. All agreed, however, that she was completely "off her head," as they put it. She hardly ever spoke about anything that made sense.

She had been there for many many years, living by herself in the derelict cottage in the company of her cat.

"I think we should find out more about old Kerry," said Richard.

"I don't really want to see old Kerry again. She frightens me. I can't get her out of my mind!"

CHAPTER 23

There is a loud, sickening crash... blackness... a sound of tearing metal... incredible heat... the sound of dripping water... people screaming... flames... children crying... many people running ... crawling... pushing... terror on their faces... railway carriages, twisted out of all proportion... people being carried out, crying, bleeding... some of them... so still...

She is running through the forest... terrified ... screaming, crying... a familiar forest... and then a woman takes her into her arms... dries her tears... brings her into a cottage deep in the woods... makes a hot water bottle for her and puts her into bed... giving her warm milk and home-made biscuits... she feels comforted... but at the same time, so lonely, so confused.

And then, the face of Kerry appears...

younger than when they saw her at the cottage . . . but just as terrifying. . .

Kerry speaks to the woman who gave her the milk . . . she points to the child . . . she is demanding something, her hand outstretched . . .

A man . . . a kind man, goes to a drawer, pulls out a sock and gives the woman a roll of banknotes. Kerry leaves . . . but she returns, again with an outstretched hand . . . again and again, each time pointing to her . . . each time receiving a roll of banknotes.

Dorothy suddenly awoke, terrified. Richard spoke to her.

"The dream again?" he asked.

"Yes," she said. "But this time I combined it somehow with our meeting with old Kerry. Everything is running together in my mind. Please go back to sleep, Richard. I am really all right. It's just our coming to this place, and old Kerry. She was so frightening."

"I think she was pathetic," said Richard. "She is only an old woman who has lost her mind. I'm sure she is harmless. We were in her house and she became upset, naturally."

"You're right," said Dorothy. "Don't worry. I'll go back to sleep." She lay back on the pillows, trying to will herself to sleep, but sleep would not come.

Here she was in Dikbos. She still hadn't found out anything, except that this seemed to be the place of the crash. But that was a step forward, surely, a massive step forward. Her parents had lived here!

Surely there was someone in the town she could speak to, someone who would remember her parents. But they had quickly found that these people from Dikbos would not talk to them. They were suspicious of them and guarded in their speech. They listened to their queries and answered in monosyllables.

ON A GOLDEN CHAIN

Dorothy suddenly felt overwhelmingly sleepy. Perhaps tomorrow they would make some sort of breakthrough.

She awoke to find Richard fully dressed inside the room.

"I've been talking to Mrs. van Rensburg," he said. "I told her a bit about what we are searching for—none of the Jewish part, of course—and she accompanied me to speak to a couple of the neighbors, the ones we tried to speak to yesterday. They do remember the crash, and they gave me all kinds of ghastly details. They were wary of speaking to you and me, since they didn't know us. Straight after the crash there had been many, many people inquiring and questioning, demanding and interrogating. The townspeople just got sick of it. They haven't forgotten, even twenty years later. Even though there were survivors, they speak as if everyone had died."

Dorothy quickly got dressed, ate some rolls and cheese and went with Richard to speak to more people. They seemed to thaw a little and gave them more information.

The crash was remembered by everyone above a certain age, but no one could give details of the passengers. Everything was one horrific, massive tragedy.

Dorothy and Richard spent the whole day this way, the people opening up to them more and more.

Some of the people living in the area described the crash in graphic detail. They added a description of the trauma the town had gone through in trying to dredge the massive coaches out of the lake. Not all the occupants had been found.

As they walked back to the guest house, the most delicious aroma greeted them—the lamb, roasted on a spit.

"What would happen if I wasn't Jewish, just for an hour?" Richard asked.

"What really stops you?" asked Mrs. van Rensberg who

had overheard. "If you want it, have it. Why hold back from something you want? Your religion can't want you to do that!"

Richard laughed. "We are eating tuna. Delicious, mouth-watering tuna!"

The next morning Dorothy could in no way be persuaded to go to the cottage in the forest. She would stay in the guest house and write letters, and Richard would try and speak to old Kerry. Perhaps she could throw light on something. She definitely would remember the train crash, if, in fact, she could remember anything. The general consensus of the whole town was that she was totally crazy and talked a string of nonsense, but perhaps she could somehow be helpful.

Old Kerry was more friendly this time and invited Richard to sit down on the settee next to the cat. He sat down uncomfortably on the couch, lumpy and scratchy where the stuffing was coming out. He wondered what his pants would look like when he got up from this mound of cat's hairs.

Old Kerry sprouted a stream of nonsense words at him which he could not understand. This went on for nearly half an hour. It was true. He would get nothing from her.

And then, quite suddenly, she addressed a question to him.

"Where is the mother of the little girl?"

Puzzled. Richard listened intently. "The little girl?" he whispered.

The woman, however, began to pour out another stream of nonsense words.

"I think I should bring Dorothy," said Richard. "Perhaps she will understand you. She is the mother of a little girl. I must bring Dorothy. You can talk to her." He left, promising to return.

Richard gently persuaded Dorothy to come back to the forest cottage with him. As the two of them approached, old Kerry came out, stick in hand.

She heaped a flow of abuse on them in several languages and then went off in some kind of gibberish.

"Let's go," whispered Richard. "No . . . wait!"

The woman was pointing at Dorothy and shouting, waving for her to go away. As they hurried down the path, Richard stopped to listen. Old Kerry was hissing out the words, "Mother, I haven't got your child. I haven't got your child and I don't know where she is. You have enough. You aren't alive, anyway. You can't be alive. The people will come back, I know, and will give me more money. We must be fair. One for one and one for one." Then she stormed back into the cottage.

At that moment, something clicked inside Dorothy's head. The dream. It hadn't been just from running into old Kerry. It had been based on fact. Her parents had lived in the cottage, and old Kerry had been blackmailing them, because she knew they had taken in the child. That is why they had left—to get away from old Kerry— to get away, perhaps, from the mother who had been searching for her child. But she had said that the mother wasn't alive. How could that be? If her mother wasn't alive, with what could she be blackmailing them?

Dorothy suddenly felt a stab of pain, not for her adoptive parents, but for her mother, her real mother, who might have been searching for her. She had to sit down.

"Richard, stop," she gasped. "I must rest for a minute. I think I figured it out." She told him her thoughts.

"I am going back to her," said Richard. "I am going back there by myself. Don't worry, she is just a noisy old woman. I don't believe she is as crazy as she sounds. It is better for me to go alone. She will talk to me eventually, I know." He brought Dorothy back to the guest house, where she promised to rest.

He walked slowly, very slowly, back to the cottage, pausing on the way to look at the moss growing under the tree, to talk to the birds and even to sit awhile to examine an ant hill.

Old Kerry watched him, her sharp eyes suspicious. She was puzzled by the young man who had time to stop and look at things. People didn't do that nowadays. People were always in a hurry. They didn't have time to stop and look and listen, and she seldom had the inclination to talk to them. Few people ever *really* listened. They were too busy planning what they were going to say next to be able to stop and listen to what was being said.

This was why no one understood her and why everyone thought she was crazy. She would admit that she was unusual, but not nearly as crazy as people imagined. Underneath was a shrewd woman, a very hurt woman, who wanted to live in peace with her cat in the forest, keeping people in fear and at bay by her gibberish and screaming.

But this young man was different. She had seen it the first time he had come. That is why she had let him sit in her living room next to her cat.

She had also been curious about him, because he knew the lady's daughter, the girl who had been stolen from her family after the train crash. Stolen? Well, not intentionally, but in a way, she was stolen. Old Kerry knew that.

She had known the childless couple who lived by themselves in the forest in the house she now occupied. She had seen them find the child running terrified through the trees after that dreadful, monstrous train crash. She shuddered at the thought. She had suffered nightmares about that crash for years.

She had seen them take the child into their home and comfort her. She had expected them to take the child back to the station, to speak to the station master, to the doctor, to anyone.

But time went on and on. The child continued to live with them, and one day she heard the child calling the woman "mama."

Kerry had gone to the people in the forest. She had told the man that she knew the child was not theirs, that she had come to them from the train crash. She had told him that a person couldn't just "take over" a child. A child had to be adopted. She told him they should go to the welfare office in the city. They were supposed to go to lawyers and social workers who could fix everything up for them.

The man had reacted with shock that anyone knew the child was with them. He had told Kerry that everyone, or nearly everyone, had died in the crash, and that the child's parents were obviously dead. No one had looked for her or come to them, and he had kept his ears open in the village for some news of parents looking for a girl her age.

"Lawyers and social workers just cause trouble," he had declared.

He had gone to a drawer, a sock, and pulled out a roll of banknotes, handing them silently to Kerry.

She had kept quiet. She was sure they would eventually go to the city and arrange things for the child, even if it took them a few more weeks. They had given her money not to report them. For a few more weeks, she would hold her peace.

But they made no moves, so she went once more to the couple. They gave her more money and again she kept quiet, and again, and again.

To Kerry this was a great deal of money, money that she

really needed to live. Keeping quiet for a while would not make any difference. Where would she get another chance to get such money?

But her conscience bothered her. One day, she decided she could take it no longer. She would go to the couple, return the money and go herself into the city and speak to the welfare office.

She had been stunned, on that day, to find the cottage deserted, all the family's belongings removed. They would be back, surely. Where could they go? And then she could speak to the welfare office.

But the family had not come back. Weeks, even months went by. Kerry's source of income had ended. She eventually moved into the deserted cottage.

Shortly afterwards, a woman had come to town searching for a little girl who had been lost since the train crash. The lady and her family had been among the badly injured, and it was months before she was discharged from the hospital. Though inquiries had been made through official channels to find the child or to ascertain what had happened to her, no news at all had come up. The woman had come, at last, to make her own inquiries.

This was the first time it had occurred to Kerry that the parents could still be alive. Hadn't everybody, almost everybody, died in the crash? But she knew this was the mother of the little girl. If only she had gone herself to the welfare office in time. Now it was too late.

She never forgot what she had done. She became obsessed with guilt, and she began to lose her mind.

And now, twenty-three years later, a young woman, looking just like the mother of the child, had come to town. This must be the child! Perhaps she could make amends. Perhaps she could lighten the stain on her soul.

She tapped the young man on the shoulder, invited him into the cottage, put together a few twigs and boiled her rusty kettle to make some coffee.

About two hours later, Richard walked out of the cottage, knowing not only the full story of the "stolen child," but also the life story of old Kerry.

She had been left an orphan after the First World War and had had to fend for herself almost all her life. At eighteen she had been engaged to be married, but her fiance had been struck by lightning. At that point she became very withdrawn. She continued to fend for herself and shunned any close relationship. She had come to the conclusion that anyone she loved would just die.

Until the Dikbos train crash, she had worked hard doing odd jobs for people, eking out a meager living. The train crash had provided her with income and a home, but it had taken its toll in guilt.

Richard now knew everything except the name of the mother. Kerry suggested that he speak to people in town. They might remember when she had come looking for her daughter.

Richard returned to Dorothy and told her everything he had gleaned from old Kerry. They decided to spend the rest of the afternoon just asking questions. They were sure their search was coming to an end.

However, it was not to be so. Many people had come to town, asking about relatives. It was impossible to pinpoint which was Dorothy's mother.

For the next two days, they questioned and queried and searched, but they got no further, except that on another visit to Kerry's cottage, Dorothy found some carvings in her father's distinctive style. At least, she had found their home.

They had gotten a lot of information from old Kerry.

ON A GOLDEN CHAIN

Richard felt he understood everything, everything, that is, except the odd song she used to sing, probably one she learned as a child, a song which she told Richard, very seriously, was the only source of comfort. No one could understand why.

"We must be fair. One for one and one for one."

CHAPTER 24

Dorothy looked out the window of the hotel in Tel Aviv at the street below. It looked like any other town. The streets were busy like any other town, but this was different. This was Israel. This was Tel Aviv.

She had been extremely excited to arrive at Lod Airport, to see the posters and signs on the wall printed in Hebrew, to hear the language in the street. It was like a dream, a beautiful, wonderful dream.

She felt incredibly at home. She had "arrived." When they made their regular call to the children and to the Kesslers, the rabbi was delighted with their reaction.

She knew she should be upset that the trail towards finding her family had somehow become lost, but at least she had found the crash and had verified her early history. It was an incredible relief to know the town in which her adoptive parents had lived, where she had spent a part of her life.

When they had returned to Johannesburg, they had spoken to people in the Jewish community to see if anyone had known about a Jewish woman searching for her daughter, but no one seemed to have been involved with the crash, if they remembered it at all. There were a fair number of Jews scattered around the rural areas in South Africa. They didn't always keep contact with the general Jewish community.

She looked back into the hotel room. Richard, completely exhausted, had already fallen asleep, his *yarmulka* beside his bed. She knew how much it had cost him to put on that *yarmulka* and walk the streets as a Jew, even though there were times when he would not wear it.

The first time he had gone to work with it, he had felt that everyone would comment and ask him about it, but *frum* Jews had worked there before, and they had accepted it without a word. She knew that whatever other hardships he was experiencing in keeping *Yiddishkeit*, this public display of his Jewishness had been the hardest.

She knew, however, that there were still times when he thoroughly resented having to do certain things. She knew he was doing many things because the *beis din* was pushing him, things which he would have added much later if not for the fact that they smoothed the way for Dorothy's and the children's conversion.

She knew he had hoped that she, and therefore the children, would be found to be Jewish and therefore not in need of conversion. Now all this had gone. Was she Jewish? Was she *really* Jewish?

She herself had sometimes felt rebellious at what the *beis din* had asked of her. A thought suddenly entered her mind.

ON A GOLDEN CHAIN

She couldn't find her family, so she was responsible to no one. Perhaps she should not convert. Where would that leave her? Free! Free to investigate other religions.

She tried to put the thought out of her mind, but it persisted. After all, here she was in Israel, in a Jewish land, in the Holy Land, holy to at least three religions. Why couldn't she visit the places sacred to all three religions? Why did she have to visit only the Jewish places? When would she have a chance to visit Israel again? Why couldn't she visit the places she had learned about in Sunday school?

She looked through the tourist guide book they had bought at the airport. They had a few ideas about where they were going, but what about including some of these places with it? And in Yerushalayim, there were so many places with artistic treasures which she would never see again.

And, of course, the Dome of the Rock. Wasn't Rabbi Kessler being a bit extreme to say that she couldn't visit it? What was wrong with going into a mosque?

Richard stirred and opened his eyes. He saw she was not in bed and then noticed her at the window. "Dorothy," he called. "You're not sleeping. What's the matter?"

"Nothing's the matter," said Dorothy. "It's just so terribly exciting being here. I just can't believe it."

Richard was pleased. He was always happy if she was happy.

She went on. "Richard, I was thinking, we should see all the holy places, not only the Jewish ones, but also the ones from other religions."

"That's fine with me," said Richard. "There's the tourist guide. You can work out the itinerary. I'm happy to go wherever you want. The book tells how to get to most places."

"That's a good idea," said Dorothy. "And I will look at the book."

She sat down at the tiny desk, poring over the book. "Richard, we could go to Caesarea tomorrow. It's an ancient Roman city with an amphitheater right by the sea. They have all kinds of Roman ruins. It's something we can't possibly miss. Then we can spend the night in Haifa and take a bus from there to wherever we want to go."

She looked at the bed. Richard was once more fast asleep. If only she had that ability, to just wake up and then go back, sound asleep.

She was still not sleepy. It was strange. Her thoughts came flooding in one after another. She was thinking of old Kerry. What a strange, odd person. She wondered what her parents had thought of her. For a moment she had a longing to speak to them. She had loved them so much. But then she began to feel uneasy. It wasn't, as she had thought, that she had been found running through forest, apparently belonging to no one. They had known she was from the train wreck, that she probably had family, and yet they had kept her. She was suddenly filled with uncomfortable feelings about them, feelings she felt guilty about, but feelings she felt she had to face. What kind of people would tear a child away from her family, away from her religion? Perhaps, in many ways, she had never really known them.

She thought of the times they had shared together. They had been good. But at all times she had been sheltered and protected. She had not been allowed to perform in school plays, and when she had been chosen to sing in a choir, they had not allowed her to do so. Had they been afraid of any public show? Did they feel so vulnerable that her real family might one day recognize her?

She remembered what her mother had said when she died about visions of her family coming to look for her. Had her adoptive parents ever met her real family? Had they hidden her and lied to her real mother? Her poor mother had gone away, desperate and empty-handed, assuming that her daughter had drowned in that vast, green lake. Dorothy shuddered at the thought. Some of the other passengers had drowned.

But why did her parents believe that she was still alive? What had made them continue to look for her?

And then she remembered. The people of Dikbos had said that many, many mothers had come to look for their children, relatives for their loved ones. Perhaps with the dead it had been easier. With the missing, would they ever cease to look?

Were they still looking? Did they ever return to Dikbos to search for her? Did they still live in South Africa?

She looked at her watch. It was two a.m. They had a long day tomorrow. Hardly had her head touched the pillow when she fell asleep.

CHAPTER

25

Dorothy woke up with a blinding headache and a feeling of impending doom. What was it that made her feel that way? Was she becoming ill?

What were they supposed to do that day? A heaviness enveloped her as she remembered. They had decided to visit the works of art in the shrines of other religions. What could be wrong with that? It was art, wasn't it? Famous pieces of artwork. What could be wrong with art and architecture?

Her headache grew more severe. Maybe she shouldn't go anywhere at all that day. Perhaps they should stay in the hotel, rest and forget about touring. They had done far too much already.

She took some aspirin and settled back on the

pillows. Richard was still asleep. It would be interesting to see some famous works of art, painting and sculpture.

She again picked up the tourist guide which gave more detailed descriptions not only of the artworks but also of the places of worship which housed them. As she read on she felt a sudden revulsion. That was not what they should do. They didn't belong in these places, no matter how famous or beautiful or magnificent the artworks were. They would not go to them.

As she looked at the guide book and at the maps, her attention was drawn to the ancient town of Safed in the north of Israel, close to the Lebanon border. Not only did Safed have an artists' village, but it was alive with Jewish history and Jewish mysticism. Her headache was beginning to clear. That's where they would go.

Richard made little comment about her change in plan. He himself had felt somewhat uncomfortable about visiting places of other religions. Safed was a much better idea, and like most places in Israel, it was accessible by bus.

Somewhat later in the day, the bus they were in began climbing upwards through an almost unending range of hills, hills and more hills. They went past Meiron, another ancient town aflame with Jewish mysticism.

The bus climbed higher and higher until Safed came into view. Dorothy had consulted the tourist guide and explained to Richard that Safed was a town with contrasting sections. There was the modern part, flaunting many hotels, which interested neither of them. There was also the old city, inhabited mostly by religious Jews and artists, intermingled in a colorful way.

Both Richard and Dorothy were deeply affected as they walked around Safed, going into the tiny *shuls* in the mysterious alleyways and courtyards.

They descended lower and lower through the ancient town until they reached the ancient cemetery and the *mikveh* of the Arizal. The graves of the *tzaddikim* were marked with blue paint of a luminous quality.

They both felt the strange, tangible stillness around the graves of the *tzaddikim*. It was as if Dorothy and Richard were alone, unaware of the many other visitors.

They were returning to the top of the ancient town through the winding alleys and twisting cobblestone paths when two boys, hardly more than five years old, with long *payos* and flying *tzitzis*, stopped in front of them and stared at Dorothy.

"Morah Miriam," one of the children said. Dorothy shook her head and kept walking. The boys suddenly seemed to realize their mistake and ran away, embarrassed, looking a little confused.

"The children are so friendly in Safed," Dorothy remarked.

Richard laughed. "I'm hungry," he said. "Where on earth are we going to find somewhere to eat?"

Dorothy suddenly spied a tiny shop, built into one of the old houses. The man behind the counter, who looked more like a rabbi than a short order cook, took their order and prepared their food. While they ate, Dorothy marvelled at how the man could function in such cramped surroundings. She had never known a quainter-looking place.

They emerged into the sunlight and made their way slowly towards the bus station. It was getting late, and they had to return to their hotel.

The following day they would be going to Yerushalayim for a stay of several days. As they drove back down through the beautiful hills, Dorothy thought how happy she was that she had chosen to go to Safed, with its labyrinth of narrow

ON A GOLDEN CHAIN

alleyways, stone staircases and archways.

There were many artworks and sculptures in Yerushalayim, she knew, but perhaps it wasn't so important to see them after all.

CHAPTER 26

The bus ride to Yerushalayim was long. Both Richard and Dorothy felt quite exhausted as they got there. Their trip to Israel was coming to a close.

As they drove through the hills, Dorothy felt her disappointment very deeply. For the first time, perhaps, she realized she had exhausted every trail. There was possibly no way her parents could be found.

Her excitement at seeing Yerushalayim for the first time banished every other thought from her mind, however. They took a taxi from the bus station and were soon in their hotel near the Old City.

They had planned to go to the Western Wall as soon as they arrived, but as they reached their hotel room and saw their comfortable, luxurious looking beds, they decided to rest, ostensibly for only half an hour.

Dorothy woke first, at four p.m. How could they have slept so long? Richard seemed to sense that she was awake and opened his eyes.

"I want to visit the Wall," said Dorothy. "I want to put a note in the Wall. I want to find my family."

"You won't now," said Richard. "There's no way."

As soon as the words escaped his lips, he felt he could have bitten off his tongue. He realized he had touched an area in Dorothy's life in which she felt really desperate. This was the end of the search. There was nothing more, nowhere to go.

She had always felt there would never be a need for herself and the children to go through a conversion process. Now, this was her only alternative.

She pulled herself together. Why should she argue with Richard? He was only stating a fact, a hard, cold fact, a fact she herself was beginning to acknowledge.

They took a taxi to the Wall and walked together towards it, both a little disappointed that there were separate areas for men and women. Perhaps it was better. Perhaps this was something which she should do alone.

She approached the Wall, noting the hundreds, thousands of notes stuck in it. She stroked one of the stones. Was this truly part of the outside wall of the *Bais Hamikdash?*

She found a piece of paper and a pen and wrote, requesting that she find her family. She folded it and put it into the Wall, wondering if anyone had ever folded a note and put it into the Wall requesting that they find *her.* It dawned on her that perhaps they hadn't given up their search. Surely, if that was so, they would one day be reunited. But again, looking at the notes, she realized the impossibility of it all.

She stopped to say *Shema* and started to walk slowly away,

knowing that she would return to this spot often, as long as she stayed in Yerushalayim. She found Richard waiting for her.

"The Dome of the Rock is over there," he said. "A lot of people seem to be going there, and a lot of them seem to be Jews. I am sure we could go with them."

"But it's a mosque! Going in there would be like worshipping another G-d," she said.

"No, it isn't," said Richard. "I am sure. They believe in only one G-d, and they don't worship anyone else."

"But we aren't allowed to go—look!" She pointed to a notice saying that Jews should not go there.

"That's strange," said Richard. "Are there notices outside all the churches where Jews are not allowed to go?"

A young man with a beard, obviously *frum*, overheard them and introduced himself as Uzi. "A Jew mustn't enter the place of worship of another faith, especially a Christian one, where the people worship other entities. But that is not the reason a Jew is not allowed to go here. Somewhere around this place is the *Kodesh Hakedoshim*, the Holy of Holies. We are not sure where it is, but it is a place so full of *kedushah* that a Jew cannot go near there. Only the High Priest went in there, only on *Yom Kippur*."

Both Richard and Dorothy were taken aback by his words, as were several Jews around them. They and several others thanked the young man and turned back and walked away. Had the notice said that? Perhaps it had. She had not even read it properly before Uzi talked to them.

"You know what?" said Dorothy, as they made their way along the beautiful, ancient pathways. "I think we should look only at the Jewish sites. I know there are famous artworks and things, but Yerushalayim is something else, beyond beautiful artworks and architecture."

There were so many Jewish sites to see that the days flew by quickly. Each day, both she and Richard went to the Wall, and each day Dorothy put a note in another part of the Wall. Perhaps by doing this, her note might be close to a note put in by her mother, and the two notes would reach Hashem together. Her feelings ranged from hope to despair, but her rationality kept telling here there was no hope. She would just have to accept it.

They booked on a tour of the Galil for two days, and a plane trip to Eilat. All too soon, however, they were boarding the plane back home.

Both Dorothy and Richard had made many decisions. They would cooperate completely with the *beis din*, Dorothy and the children would convert, but at the same time, they would write to various *batei din* and Jewish newspapers. But they could wait no longer. What if she didn't find her family for another five or ten years? What if she never found them?

They would have to be realistic. They would become totally observant and would do everything expected of them.

And so it continued for several months. The time for the conversion was approaching fast.

CHAPTER
27

The street was quiet. It was generally a quiet street and a quiet time of day. There was very little traffic in either direction.

Lucy and Steven were ambling along the sidewalk, each weighed down on one side by their heavy bookbags. It always felt good to be out of school, and they found the walk home far more pleasant than what seemed like the longer walk to school. They chatted happily about the lessons they had had, the things they had done at recess and the projects the art teacher had given their respective classes to do. They did not take much notice of the five bigger boys who suddenly appeared in front of them.

"Hey, Jew-boy," the roughest looking boy said, looking nastily at the two children.

Steven just nodded uncertainly and tried to

pass. The other boys barred his way, ignoring Lucy.

"What's that silly beanie you're wearing, Jew boy?" asked the first boy again. "It doesn't match your face. Let's make it match your face."

He turned to his friends. One of them aimed a blow at Steven's nose. Steven felt a sharp pain go through him and he tasted blood in his mouth. He made a move to go. Lucy stood there as if paralyzed. She didn't want to leave her brother, yet she knew she had to run for help. She reasoned that she would not be much help to him where she was. She would only get attacked herself.

Hopefully, her father would be home. He often came home early on Mondays. She sped off at top speed, trying to force the awareness out of her mind that one of the boys had thrown Steven to the ground and that the others had started kicking him.

She arrived home, crying and trembling. Richard, opening the door, could see immediately that something dreadful had happened.

"It's Steven," she said, "Come quickly. They are trying to kill him!"

Richard outran her to the place she indicated. He could see the boys, and he ran faster. One of them turned and saw him approaching, and the five quickly disappeared, leaving a dazed and wounded Steven lying on the ground.

Richard knelt beside him, aware that he himself had tears in his eyes. Steven had a black eye, and blood was streaming from his nose. He had red marks over his legs and arms where he had been kicked. His lip was cut and swollen.

Richard picked him up, cradling him in his arms as if he were a baby.

"What happened, Stevie?" he kept repeating over and over.

Steven said nothing. He just kept whimpering that his head and legs were sore. Lucy finally caught up with him. She took one look at her brother and burst out crying.

"He's alive still, isn't he, Dad? He's alive still?"

"Yes, of course he is," said her father reassuringly. "I want you to rush home and tell Mummy to call the doctor urgently. I will bring him home in a few minutes."

"Will he be all right?" asked Lucy.

"Yes, yes, I am sure he will," said Richard. He started to walk home with him, still carrying him like a baby.

"They called me a Jew-boy," said Steven, amidst his sobs. "They called me a Jew-boy and then started hitting me and kicking me."

Richard stood still, feeling as if an icy hand had just grasped his heart and held it tight.

What had he done to his son? What had he allowed to happen to his family? He himself had known what anti-Semitism meant, and he had allowed his son to bear the brunt of it. He felt his head beginning to pound and a sick, empty feeling hit his stomach.

"I'm sorry, Stevie," he whispered. "I am sorry. I can never, ever tell you how sorry I am. But it isn't too late, my baby. No one is going to hurt you again. No one will hurt you *ever* again."

He had reached his home, and Dorothy was coming to meet them. She gasped as she saw Steven.

"I've called the doctor," she said. "He's coming right away. In the meanwhile, we will try to wash off all this blood."

She started to sponge the child, wiping his face very gently. He whimpered slightly.

"Stevie, what happened?" she asked.

"They called him a Jew-boy," said Richard in an oddly calm tone, a tone which sent a shiver down her spine. She did not ask him anything further. She didn't want to hear what he would say.

There was a ring at the door. The doctor had arrived. He examined Steven carefully. Steven allowed him to do this until he touched his left leg, which was obviously giving him a lot of pain. The doctor reassured him and examined it gently, making sure that nothing was broken.

"He's all right," he said, straightening up. "He will have some interesting looking bruises, but there is nothing really serious. I suggest a hot bath, some Tylenol and a very, very early night. And no school tomorrow."

"He won't be going back to that school," said Richard. "He's staying at home."

"A bit young to stop a person's education," said the doctor, smiling. "Keep him home till the weekend and then decide. It's almost school holidays, anyway. I think you have all had a very big shock."

He shook Richard's hand and then he left. Richard walked stiffly back into the house.

"This is the end," he said to Dorothy. "I have to make some moves, some decisions, but this is the end. I think this Jewish thing is going to have to stop and to stop here and now. I am taking some leave, and if they don't give it to me I will work somewhere else. We might even leave altogether. But we are going away from this place. We are going somewhere far away for a holiday, away from Jews and Judaism and anti-Semitism. I've just got to get away from everything *frum* or Jewish. I have to think about all this. What are we exposing our children to?"

CHAPTER 28

Any other time it would have been good to go away to the northern coast. Such a trip would have filled the family with a sense of excitement.

Now, as they travelled, each was busy with his or her own thoughts. Each felt a certain tension and confusion.

Richard, who was driving, had felt for several days that his world was somehow splitting apart. He had had many doubts and resistance to *Yiddishkeit*, and a lot of these had been solved. Over the last few months, Judaism had been becoming truly meaningful to him. He had found Rabbi Kessler's approach very inspiring.

When Steven had been attacked, it was as if a very cold, steel dagger had gone right through him. The words of Rev. Purdy had come back to him again and again. What was he doing to his children, these innocent children?

After the incident with Steven, Richard had gone to see Rabbi Kessler and had spoken to him, but he himself realized he had put up between them an impenetrable barrier. He did not want to be Jewish, or if he did, he couldn't be, for the sake of his children.

But as soon as he thought about this, about a life without *Yiddishkeit*, he felt within himself a terrible emptiness, as though everything had become without taste or color. But for his children's sake, he had to break away.

In the meanwhile, they were going to the coast, to a quiet village, to a place where they could all be together and think.

Dorothy had been especially shocked by the anti-Semitic attack on her son. For the first time since she had found the small Jewish star on the golden chain, she had serious doubts about what she was doing. Was the attack a surprise? Hadn't she read about anti-Semitism? Hadn't the book she had read so long ago made it obvious that anti-Semitism was still rife in the world? Did she really want it for her children? Wouldn't it be better to be free?

She began to fantasize that they would drive up to a roadhouse, and all of them would order bacon and eggs for breakfast, with cocoa to go with it. They would eat it like any other gentile family. But then in her mind she would see her two children looking at her with their large, trusting eyes. Could she do this to them? Could she deliberately give them non-kosher food? What would she be doing to their Jewish souls?

She steeled herself. Did they *have* Jewish souls? There was no real evidence that she was Jewish. The *beis din* was not even remotely satisfied with anything she had told them about this. She and her children were to go through a conversion like any gentile wanting to become Jewish, and according to this, she wasn't Jewish yet, and neither were the children.

She couldn't find her family, so she had no responsibility to anyone except her husband and her children. How could she allow her children to be persecuted because they were Jewish? For the sake of her husband and her family, they had to forget the whole thing.

She came out of her reverie and reached over to the bag in which she had everyone's kosher sandwiches. It would soon be time for breakfast.

Steven felt somehow responsible for the change in attitude in his home. He wished he had never told his father he had been called a Jew-boy. He was still quite sore in several places, and the bruises were becoming a yellowish, blackish green. He was very conscious of his black eye and was relieved that he hadn't been forced to return to school. He would have had too much explaining to do.

He told himself that he should be excited about the holiday at Carroll Beach, and perhaps he was, in a way. But he had that awful empty feeling, a feeling that something had gone terribly wrong.

Lucy was angry. Her world had been messed up. She had been told that she was no longer allowed to play with Leah and Bluma and Dina, and her parents were talking about leaving the town, their friends and even their Judaism. And it was all Steven's fault.

All right, he did get attacked, and she had been extremely worried about him, especially when she thought that something dreadful had happened to him. But why did he have to tell their father it was because he was a Jew? It was Steven who had caused all this. She stared glumly out of the window.

Both children were not quite sure what was happening in their home, and they were not at all sure they liked what was happening.

ON A GOLDEN CHAIN

They had been overjoyed when they had heard that they would be going for a coastal holiday and that they would be staying in one of the beachfront holiday apartments. They had been excited as their mother had helped them pack their clothes, and as they had helped her pack the frozen food to be transferred to the freezer as soon as they arrived. They had enjoyed trying to fit in the double hot plate, kettle, dishes, cups, glasses and cutlery. It seemed that they were really taking their kitchen on holiday with them.

But from the time they had gotten into the car, there had been a sadness in their mother, and a desperation and an almost aggressive determination in their father which they could not understand. After all, a holiday was a holiday. Surely their parents should be happy.

They were also feeling very tired, and they started to fall asleep in the back of the car.

Richard drove on, his mouth set in a grim, determined scowl. Was this "Jewish thing" worth it all? What gains were there really for his family? Why should he let Rabbi Kessler dictate what he should eat and what he should not eat?

Who was Rabbi Kessler, anyway? He was from the dark ages—someone who had been brought up in the traditions of his parents, grandparents and great-grandparents, who had never had the intellectual honesty to examine his beliefs critically.

His feelings of bitterness and disillusionment increased as he entertained these thoughts in his mind. Rabbi Kessler had tried to force his archaic religion onto them, to force him and his wife, intelligent, educated people, to live a restricted, meaningless life. He was happy he would not see the Kesslers again, and though he didn't actually *feel* happy about it, he was sure that somewhere or other he was happy.

He usually enjoyed driving, but he wasn't really enjoying

this. Dorothy noticed his discomfort and looked at him reassuringly.

"We can always go back to the Kesslers if it doesn't work out," she said.

His face went red. "Never!" he exclaimed. "I'll never go back to them. I will never have anything to do with their type of Jews and Judaism. I can see why everyone hates them! They think they are different and better, but all they are is hopelessly out of date, worshipping a G-d who spends His time peering into people's pots in the kitchen, and condemning them, and interfering in general with their lives."

"Would you like a G-d who was so far away and distant that He didn't care what you are doing, and anything you did, good or bad, wouldn't make a difference?" asked Dorothy.

"Let's not talk about it," said Richard. "Let's forget about it. We will go on our holiday, and when we come back we'll decide whether we will become Presbyterian again."

Dorothy was silent for a few minutes. "Can you believe all that again?" she whispered.

"No, of course not," he said, his voice sounding irritated. "But I'm sure half or even three-quarters of the people who go to church take most of it with a grain of salt. It's important as a kind of social thing, a sort of club, as it were. You go in, sit for an hour, sing a few hymns, go outside and chat to your friends and acquaintances and go home."

Dorothy's feelings of emptiness became overwhelming. She sighed from the depths of her being.

Richard looked at her sharply. "Don't let all this spoil our holiday. Let's just be happy. We were happy once, before all this happened. We had everything we wanted, a good home, good friends, a nice, balanced moderate community. We were good gentile people."

Dorothy felt nauseous. She could never again be satisfied

with that. Contact with *Yiddishkeit* had opened up depths within her which were satisfied only by *Yiddishkeit*. These depths were still opened and feeling empty. It would take time before she could be happy. She *would* be happy. Rabbi Kessler had said that a person could be happy in any situation if they made an effort to be happy. She would try to do this. She would pull herself together, pretend there were no tears in her eyes and be happy.

"How many more hours is it before we reach the sea?" she asked.

"About four and a half," he replied. "It's a beautiful beach, but somewhat deserted because the bathing is difficult, too many rocks and unexpected currents. But we are not there for the swimming. The children can paddle in the shallow waves. This will be the most wonderful holiday we have ever had, just on our own with no one who knows us."

They travelled on and on, putting miles and miles between themselves and the life they had been leading. No one knew what they were doing. No one, not even Rabbi Kessler knew what they were considering. Or did he have some idea?

The last time they had seen him, he had looked at them in a strange, intense way. Could he have known what they would do?

Dorothy felt her spirits rising as she saw the vast expanse of blue shimmering in the distance. The sea! How she loved the sea! She had delighted in it ever since she was a child.

"Lucy! Steven! Wake up!" she said. "We can see the sea."

The children woke excitedly, responding to their mother's tone, and they started to discuss all kinds of plans.

"I am sure there will be other children to play with," said Lucy.

"Not many," said Richard. "This is a very quiet part of the coast. It is very beautiful, but not all that popular. But I am sure we will find a few children about. Even if there aren't, we will be doing all kinds of things together, and we'll have a really great holiday."

Eventually they approached the tiny coastal village of Carroll Beach, which consisted of one hotel, several blocks of holiday apartments and some holiday cottages. There were also homes for about a hundred and fifty families and, of course, a small shopping center.

They drove up to a quiet, whitewashed apartment building and were soon unpacking their provisions.

"We'll have to do something to this kitchen to make it more kosher," said Richard, forgetting his rebellion as he set about to tackle the problem.

He looked into the chest freezer and dropped in the half frozen meat, bread and milk.

"Actually, it won't take that much," he said. "We have our own hot plates for meat, and we won't have anything hot that's *mil chig* except coffee and cocoa, and we have a kettle."

Dorothy and the children were relieved at the way he was talking. Not until much later, when the children were asleep and they had been working for a long time, did he turn to Dorothy with his old aggression.

"Do you know how much easier it would have been to be able to move into the hotel and just eat out for all our meals? But of course, there's nothing kosher anywhere near this place. Dorothy, oh Dorothy, we have to decide if this is going

CHAPTER
29

*T*o be the life for our children!"

That *Shabbos* evening the Wilson family was sitting somewhat disconsolately over the *Shabbos* meal. It just wasn't like *Shabbos*.

It wasn't only that they were away from the Kesslers, away from their home and their *shul*. Under any other circumstances, it would have been fun to eat a *Shabbos* meal next to a large window which looked straight onto the sea, the waves a deep indigo, very clear under the full moon. It would have been wonderful to keep *Shabbos* in such beautiful surroundings.

But Richard and Dorothy had become tense and aggressive with one another, and the children had reacted to this with an increase in their own confusion and anger.

From the moment that *Shabbos* had begun,

discord had increased, as if the ushering in of a day of *kedushah* brought out everything negative within the family.

Richard had watched his wife light the *Shabbos* candles, a sullen expression on his face. His response had immediately been, "Now we are trapped within our own holiday apartment. Now there's nothing we can do. We can't do this and can't do that. We can't even watch television." He had stared accusingly at the television.

"I am not sure how long the family will carry on with this," he had continued darkly. "I don't know if we will really pursue this Jewish thing." He had then picked up a novel and read it until it was time for the meal.

He had made *kiddush* in a flat, uninspired way. They had all washed and said *Hamotzi*, and as soon as they were all able to speak again, Richard had said, "Do you know what? This might be the last time this family ever keeps *Shabbos*."

His statement was received in stunned silence. Richard had then brought his novel to the table and carried on reading, occasionally giving a growl if anyone interrupted him.

"You can't just make a statement like that," said Dorothy, trying to take him out of his book. "And how can you read at the *Shabbos* table, and a novel at that?"

Richard glared at her. "What else is there to do on *Shabbos*?" he asked. "*Shabbos* has no meaning any more. Next week, we will go to the beach on *Shabbos*."

"But we must keep *Shabbos*," said Lucy almost in a whisper. "We are Jewish."

Richard turned on her. "Oh no, you aren't," he said. "Do you think the *beis din* accepts you children or your mother as Jewish? You all have to be converted. If they saw you as Jewish, you wouldn't have to do that. They see you as gentiles, as Presbyterian. Gentiles don't have to keep *Shabbos*, and they don't have to hold back from eating lobsters and crayfish and all those delicacies."

"Those always gave you heartburn," said Dorothy. "You said long before Nana died that you had to stop eating them."

"Not any more," said Richard. "My heart no longer burns."

He was silent, and as he looked at his daughter he found that she was crying.

"Lucy, my baby," he said. "Your brother got badly beaten up because he was wearing a *yarmulka*. I'm not going to expose my children to hurt or danger. I want you all to be happy and safe. I am doing it for your sakes. Look what happened to your brother!"

Lucy went over to Steven and punched him hard. "It's all your fault," she said.

Steven punched back. Soon there was screaming, hair pulling, kicking and scrambling on the floor.

"Lucy, Steven, don't fight like that. It's *Shabbos*," Dorothy burst out. "You'll hurt one another."

"But Daddy said it was going to be just like any other day, like Monday or Tuesday or Thursday. It's not going to be special anymore," said Lucy. "So what's the difference if we fight on *Shabbos* or not?"

"Other things will be special," Richard said.

"What other things?" asked Lucy. "Where else can you have *Kiddush* and *challah* and *bentching* and *Havdalah* and *cholent* and everything else about *Shabbos*?"

The children were becoming more and more despondent.

"Richard, leave them alone. You are upsetting them," said Dorothy. "You don't have to make such a thing about it."

"Dorothy," he said quietly. "They will get used to this. I think it will be a relief to them to be free again from all the restrictions. Just give them time. A child naturally wants freedom."

"I heard you, Daddy," said Lucy. "I heard you. We do want *Shabbos*. It was such fun with Bluma and Shlomo and Dina and Leah."

"You'll find other friends," said Richard. "You will have fun with them."

Richard sat quietly, reflecting, looking miserable.

"Dot," he said at last. "I think we must make a completely new start, even, perhaps, in a new country. We must go away from the Kesslers, far away. We must even go away from Rev. Purdy. We will just be normal people, leading normal lives."

Shabbos day dawned and with it a little optimism. The sun was shining, and the sea was a sparkling blue.

The family decided to go for a walk along the beach. The heavy atmosphere of the previous night had been pushed aside.

The *Shabbos* midday meal was also more pleasant for all concerned. It was as if there had been an agreement amongst the whole family not to bring up any kind of controversial subject, certainly not anything to do with *Yiddishkeit*.

Straight after the meal, however, Richard got up, announcing that he was going to visit his friends next door.

"But, it's *Shabbos*," said Dorothy in surprise. "Those people aren't Jewish."

"That's why I am going there," said Richard. "The McLeans are Scottish, they aren't Jewish, and Bob McLean is a soccer fan. He will have the television on. He, a non-Jew, will have put it on, so there is no problem for me to watch it."

"But you can't do that," said Dorothy. "It isn't right. It's *Shabbos*."

"But I am not *doing* anything, Dorothy," he said. "All I am doing is walking to my door, opening it, walking to his door, without carrying anything, knocking at his door, walking in and sitting down in a chair. What have I done then?"

"Nothing, if you put it that way," said Dorothy. "Except that the whole thing is against the spirit of *Shabbos*."

"It's an important game," said Richard, walking to the door. "A lot depends on this game."

And with that he was gone.

There is a loud, sickening crash . . . blackness . . . a sound of tearing metal . . . incredible heat . . . the sound of dripping water . . . people screaming . . . flames . . . children crying . . . many people running . . . crawling . . . pushing . . . terror on their faces . . . railway carriages, twisted out of all proportion . . . people being carried out, crying, bleeding . . . some of them . . . so still . . . people are lying side by side alongside the tracks . . . children . . . She looks into one of their faces . . . her face, except that it is covered in blood . . . she screams . . .

She is running through a forest . . . dark, tall trees . . . she is screaming and screaming . . .

Richard awoke at about four a.m. to hear Dorothy screaming and screaming.

"Dorothy, Dorothy, stop that," said Richard. "People will think I am attacking you or something. It's your dream again."

"Richard, I can't bear it," she said, crying. "It is so much worse now that I know it is true. This will always be with me. It was so real. I was there, standing, looking at myself, and I was lying there, full of blood. Then I ran away into the Dikbos forest, screaming and screaming."

"You sure were," said Richard.

"I think it's worse, also," said Dorothy, "now that I know

we have given up searching for my parents. I will never, ever work this thing out. I will never, ever know the truth."

"Maybe that is better," said Richard. "We tried everything we could, more than everything we should, and we have come up with nothing. Except the part about South Africa," he admitted. "You found out where your adoptive parents came from."

"But I don't know who I am," said Dorothy. "And I don't know who my children are! We don't belong anywhere. We don't belong anywhere at all."

CHAPTER

30

Here was truly a magnificent sand castle, far bigger than most sand castles. In fact, it was becoming big enough for a child to sit inside and look out through the turrets. The Shulman children had been working on it for more than two hours, and it was certainly becoming a masterpiece.

Batsheva was busy making sure that each of the turrets had been clearly marked. Her designs were almost like brickwork.

Alex was straightening out the walls, at the same time trying to deepen the moat to be ready to be filled with water. Menachem and Yosef were busy searching for shells and seaweed to add to the decorations.

A short distance away from them, their father Rabbi Yisrael Shulman was sitting on a large boulder. He looked up from his *sefer* to watch the waves as they came in and broke against the shore, forcing the water back with the heavy backwash to return once more in a cascade of deep emerald, turquoise and white foam.

He had chosen an isolated part of an isolated beach and everything was quiet around them. The Shulmans had arrived on the previous day, and the family had spent many hours *kashering* their holiday cottage kitchen, making it ready for use. Now they could relax.

The children were happy with their castle. They had worked hard on it and were proud of it. The rabbi wondered how long it would last.

It was no wonder that Lucy and Steven, seeing it from a distance, ran over to it and were soon introducing themselves to the Shulman children.

"Can we help you?" asked Steven. "Lucy can model quite well. She always does with clay."

Batsheva and Alex moved over, making room for them. Steven was given the job of fetching water in the bucket to fill up the moat. They were so busy that they worked together as if they had known one another for years.

"Why have you got so many bruises?" asked Batsheva, looking at Steven curiously. "Did you get hurt?"

"Someone hit me," said Steven. "Some bigger boys."

"That's awful," said Alex. "Didn't your big brother beat them up?"

"I haven't got a big brother," said Steven simply.

"Oh, we have," said Alex. "And we have bigger sisters, but they are all away at camp."

"Have you been here long?" asked Batsheva. "We only arrived yesterday."

"Only a few days," said Steven. "But it was awful because there were hardly any children here."

"We are here now," said Alex.

"We can't stay here too long," said Lucy. "Mummy and Daddy will be worried if we are away for too long. We are actually on the way to the shops." She pointed to the basket, but was again soon engrossed in digging out dungeons beneath the castle.

"Are you Jewish?" asked Menachem, looking at Steven.

Steven blushed.

"Do I look Jewish?" he asked.

"I don't know," said Menachem. "I just wondered if you were."

"No, we are not," said Lucy. "We are Presbyterian and we are going to eat pork and bacon and all kinds of *treif* things. We aren't going to keep *Shabbos*, and in fact, we will drive and keep the television on and do everything that a non-Jew does."

The Shulman children nodded, accepting this. Only Rabbi Shulman raised his eyebrows and looked with interest at the two children before he went back to his learning. That had certainly been a very strange answer coming from a child who claimed not to be Jewish. In fact, it would be a strange answer coming from anyone.

As a school principal, he had an awareness and a perception of the soul of a child, which comes only from dedication, love and experience.

Lucy once again stated that she had to go to the shops and back to her parents, but she said they would come back and play again.

"Before you go," said the rabbi. "Tell me where you are staying. Maybe we can fetch you to go with us one day for a picnic."

"That would be lovely," said Steven excitedly. "But you have to ask my dad. His name is Mr. Wilson, and we are staying at the Seaview, apartment 214."

"Thank you, young man," said the rabbi, giving him the smile which had caught the hearts of so many of his pupils.

For a few moments, Steven stared at him. Even though this man had red hair and a red beard, and even though he was very casually dressed, there was something about him that reminded him of Rabbi Kessler. But this couldn't be so.

His parents had said they were going to a place where there were no Jews. No, he couldn't be Jewish. He wasn't wearing a *yarmulka*. He was wearing a fisherman's cap, and the boys were wearing sun-caps. However, they all wore *tzitzis* as the Kesslers did. Maybe it wasn't only Jews who did that.

Lucy tapped her brother, and they were soon on their way to the shops.

"We can play with them again tomorrow," said Lucy. "Batsheva is nice, really nice."

"And we can go for a picnic with them," said Steven. "Only I said he had to ask Daddy."

"They also have a baby sister," said Lucy. "Batsheva was telling me, a baby sister called Chaya."

"I like them," said Steven. "I am so glad there are some children over here. I felt good with them. They reminded me a bit of the Kesslers."

"That's right," said Lucy, puzzled. "I wonder if they could be Jewish!"

"They are lucky if they are," said Steven. "They would be so lucky to have *Shabbos* and *Yom Tov* and *berachos* and all that forever and ever."

"But Steven!" exclaimed Lucy. "You got beaten up badly, beaten up because you looked like a Jew. We can't be Jewish. People are too much against the Jews. It isn't good for us."

"It is well worth being beaten up a hundred times if we could be really Jewish," said Steven. "I hate being a gentile, and Mummy and Daddy are unhappy, too. I twice found Mummy crying, and when I got near her, she said she had a cold. And Daddy has been so cross and irritable. He never smiles, and he won't talk to me at all. He says we are all enjoying ourselves, but he doesn't seem to even enjoy watching football any more. Even though we are doing all sorts of things this holiday, it isn't all that nice."

"Do you think Mummy and Daddy are happy being gentiles?" asked Lucy.

"No," said Steven very definitely.

"Well, it's your fault that they are," said his sister nastily. "If you hadn't come home and said that those boys had called you a Jew-boy and beaten you up, you wouldn't have started all this."

"But they hit me so hard, and they kicked me," said Steven. "I had to tell Mummy and Daddy what happened."

"But you could have left out the bit about the Jew-boy," said Lucy.

"What shall we do?" asked Steven. "Shall we phone the Kesslers?"

"Don't be silly," said Lucy. "It would cost more than both our allowances, and we need that to buy sweets. And Mummy and Daddy said that they never, ever wanted to see the Kesslers again."

"I'll tell you what," said Steven, unable to forget the way the children's father at the beach had looked at them. "If the Shulmans are Jewish, maybe we could go over and talk to them."

"Maybe we won't," said Lucy. "Maybe they aren't Jewish. Why should they be?"

"We'll ask them," said Steven.

"How can you do that?" asked Lucy. "Maybe they will get cross."

"Menachem asked me," said Steven, "and you answered him."

"That's right," said Lucy. "Maybe we can ask them then, and if they start to get cross, then we can just say we are asking them because they were asking us."

"Why were you children so long?" asked Dorothy. "We were getting really worried. I knew your father shouldn't have sent you by yourselves. You probably got lost or something."

Both Steven and Lucy flinched, not so much at their mother's words, but rather at the tone of her voice. They had never, ever known her to be so consistently angry and upset.

"We helped some friends build a sandcastle," said Lucy.

"I think we will go and help them again tomorrow," said Steven.

"Which friends?" asked Dorothy. "Did you find someone to play with at last?"

"Three boys and a girl, and the eldest boy Alex is exactly Steven's age and the girl is not more than a year or two younger than me."

"But we haven't met them," Dorothy began.

"Dorothy!" shouted Richard. "You can't wrap those children up in cotton wool. They have found friends. Let them play with them!"

Dorothy gave an exaggerated sigh. "It's on your head," she said.

"You have been overprotecting them ever since Steven got beaten up," said Richard. "We are no longer going to be Jews. He is in no danger. No one is going to beat him up again. No one can be anti-Semitic to someone who isn't Jewish. Don't worry so much."

The children slipped quietly into their room, took out

their pencil crayons and coloring books, and were soon busy making the characters more fierce than even the artist had intended.

"Mummy and Daddy never used to fight like that," said Steven. "Never, ever. No one is happy any more."

"We are," said Lucy. "In a way, and one should be happy at the sea."

"Yes," said Steven miserably. "But I don't like being a gentile by the sea."

"That's true," said Lucy. "Tomorrow, then, we will try and do something about it."

"And if the Shulmans aren't Jewish?" asked Steven.

"Then we'll think of something else," said Lucy. "Perhaps they might tell us where to find someone Jewish."

They whispered all the way through supper and all the way to their room, going to bed quite early.

Both Dorothy and Richard were too involved in their own arguments to even notice that the children had gone to bed unusually early, with a great deal of whispering.

"I am going to say *Shema* before I go to bed," said Lucy.

"I never stopped doing that," said Steven. "But I was too scared even to tell you."

CHAPTER 31

Very early the next morning, Steven and Lucy were ready to go for a walk along the beach to find their friends. They went straight to the place where the castle had been and were disappointed to find that part of the turret had caved in, and the patterns carefully drawn by Batsheva had almost completely disappeared. The Shulmans were nowhere to be seen.

"They will come soon, I am sure," said Steven. "Let's fix up the castle and wait for them."

Lucy agreed, and they worked hard for almost an hour.

"They aren't here," said Steven disconsolately. "They said they were going to a picnic and that maybe we could go, too, but they have gone without us."

"It's still very early," said Lucy. "Perhaps..."

She gave a cry of delight as she saw Batsheva running towards her.

"Lucy, Steven," she called out. "We were wondering if you would be here. Mummy is waiting over there with the pram with Chayele in it. We were going to the shop, and I wondered if you would be here. Come and see my baby sister and my mother."

The children were soon introduced to Mrs. Feige Shulman and Chayele who looked at them carefully with her large, blue eyes.

"She's lovely, just lovely!" said Lucy. "She's like a doll. She's so pretty."

Lucy and Steven were soon invited to the Shulman's holiday cottage. They would not be going to the beach for at least another hour.

"But I think we should tell your parents first," said Feige Shulman. "I am sure they would like to know where you are."

Lucy and Steven immediately agreed, and they were soon standing, together with Feige Shulman and her children, outside the Wilson's hotel room door.

Dorothy answered the knocking and agreed that the children could go to the cottage. She liked the look of Mrs. Shulman. Besides being undeniably beautiful, she had a directness and a warmth which drew Dorothy to her instinctively. It never actually occurred to her that Feige Shulman was Jewish, though she could have figured out by the way she was dressed that she was a *frum* Jewish woman.

She asked if the children could be back for lunch, and Feige agreed.

Rabbi Shulman had discussed with his wife the strange answer Lucy had given when asked if they were Jewish, and Feige had hoped to throw some light on the matter in her meeting with Dorothy. It had been far too brief, however, and she had returned as mystified as ever.

Some fifteen minutes later, Steven and Lucy were seated at the Shulman's table, eating hot buttered scones. Alex, Menachem and Yosef had been delighted to see them. They really liked the friends they had met at the beach, even though they weren't Jewish.

Rabbi Shulman was not with them. He had been *davening* in the lounge. As soon as he had finished, however, he came into the room, still wearing *tallis* and *tefillin*.

Lucy and Steven stared at him, both growing a bright red.

Rabbi Shulman smiled. "These are *tefillin*," he said, pointing to them.

"I know," said Lucy. "But tell me, does that mean that you are Jewish?"

"I am," said the rabbi. "So is all my family. Are *you* Jewish?"

"No," said Steven. "I mean, maybe. We nearly were, and now we aren't."

"We think we may be Presbyterian now, even though we don't believe in any of it," said Lucy. "But we won't be eating kosher and we are going to break *Shabbos*."

Rabbi Shulman looked at them encouragingly. There were a million questions he wanted to ask them, but he knew that most children respond to interrogation with negativity. He would just have to wait.

"I didn't make a *brachah* before I ate this scone," said Steven. "That's because I am a gentile."

"Do you like being a gentile?" asked Alex.

Steven felt his eyes filling with tears. How embarrassing. He couldn't cry! Not in front of these people! He took out a tissue and blew his nose hard. Lucy glared at him.

"Would you two like to talk to me in the other room?" asked the rabbi.

Relieved, Steven quietly went into the lounge, followed

by Lucy and the rabbi who had, on the way, picked up two large glasses of orange juice. He turned to Steven.

"You make a *berachah* on that if you want to, even if you are a gentile," he said.

Both children immediately did that and took a sip of the juice.

"Not a bad *berachah* for two children who aren't Jewish," he said.

Lucy smiled.

"Would you like to tell me something about all this?" said the rabbi as casually as he could.

"Yes," said Steven. "Lucy and I talked about it last night. We decided that if you are Jewish, we were going to talk to you."

"I'm Jewish," he said. "But what made you think I might be Jewish?"

"I don't know," said Lucy. "It is just that you reminded us of someone, a rabbi."

"Do I look like him?" asked Rabbi Shulman.

"No," said Lucy. "I mean, in a way, yes. But you have a red beard and red hair and green eyes. And Rabbi Kessler has black hair and brown eyes and he is very tall."

"So in what way are we alike?" the rabbi asked, making a mental note to contact Rabbi Kessler, whom he had met once at a conference.

"I don't know," said Lucy. "It was just something."

"Do you want to tell me what it's all about?" asked the rabbi again.

"It's a long story," said Steven. "It all started on the day I got my toy train. It was Lucy's birthday. She got a doll, a really nice doll, as dolls go, and she called her Esther. And the train frightened my mother because she has always been scared of trains."

The rabbi looked from one child to another.

"Go on," he said.

"Well," said Lucy. "That night my grandmother died, and she said, I mean, I think she said, because Mummy never told us directly, but we heard everyone talking. She said that Mummy wasn't really her daughter and that she had been found as a little girl, after a train crash and that she had around her neck a star on a golden chain. It was a small Jewish star."

Rabbi Shulman was beginning to understand, but he did not interrupt.

"And then," said Steven, "Mummy looked all over for her parents, but she didn't know where they were or how to find them. They looked at one train crash and it was the wrong one, and then they looked at another one, far, far away in South Africa. It seemed to be the right one, but they still couldn't find out who Mummy's parents were. And no one knows if she is Jewish or not."

Steven paused.

"What about your father?" asked the rabbi.

"Well, you see, his mother was Jewish before she married my grandfather and became Presbyterian, so he is a bit Jewish."

"Completely," said the rabbi.

"No," said Steven. "He isn't any more. He is Presbyterian again and he is going to eat *treif* now and he isn't going to keep *Shabbos*, and he is very, very cross about it."

"How did you meet Rabbi Kessler?" asked the rabbi.

"Mummy phoned and we all went to see him and we all liked him," said Lucy. "We loved Bluma and Leah and Rivki and everyone."

"Mummy and Daddy spoke to him a lot, but there were times that we didn't see them for a long time and there were times we weren't allowed to talk to them," said Steven.

"And Mummy was going to the *beis din* and we also went once," said Lucy. "But then Steven spoiled it all."

The boy turned crimson and bit his lip.

"What happened, Steven?" asked the rabbi gently, his eyes seeming to search the child's very soul.

"I got beaten up," said Steven. "I got beaten up on the way home from school. I was wearing a *yarmulka* and they called me a Jew-boy. They hit me and punched me and kicked me, so Lucy ran home and called my father. When he came, all the boys ran away. Then he asked me what happened."

"You shouldn't have told him," said Lucy. "If you hadn't told him, we would still be Jewish, or almost Jewish."

Steven found hot tears running down his cheeks.

"I wouldn't mind being hit like that again and again if only I could be Jewish," he said amidst his sobbing.

All the time Rabbi Shulman had been listening to the children, he had become more and more convinced that they were Jewish. Now he had no doubts, but he knew that a strong feeling would not, and in fact, should not, hold water with a *beis din*. Either the family had to convert, or Dorothy's parents or their family had to be found.

"When did you get beaten up?" he asked.

"It's only about three weeks ago," said Steven.

"We haven't really broken *Shabbos* yet, but we will next week, and we are going to start to eat *treif*."

"Are your parents happy about it?" asked the rabbi.

"No," said Lucy and Steven together.

Lucy continued. "They are very, very unhappy and very, very cross with everyone. It is terrible!"

"Can I go and see them?" asked the rabbi.

"Are you a rabbi?" asked Steven. "They will be very cross if you are a rabbi."

"Well, I'm not a rabbi of a *shul*," he said. "I work in a school."

"I suppose that's okay," said Steven.

"I am worried," said Lucy. "I am worried that they might get very, very cross with you, and then you won't want us to come here again."

"No chance of that," said the rabbi, thinking to himself that if he could cope with some of the parents of his school, he could cope with anyone.

"But maybe they will stop us coming to you," said Lucy.

The rabbi could not deny that this was possible.

"We will talk to them when we take you home," he said. "In the meanwhile, let's go and see how our sand castle is. It should be safe. No one seems to go to that part of the beach because of the rocks. It is totally impossible to swim there. Which makes it all the better for us," he added.

CHAPTER 32

Richard stiffened and then whitened as he opened the door to the Shulmans. He had no illusions. The man in front of him was obviously a religious Jew. Was this a vision sent to taunt him? Here he was, in Carroll Beach, a small seaside town. Why should a religious Jew be here? And how had the children become friendly with his family?

On the other hand, the man probably did not know they had any connection with Judaism. He was just the father of two children who had met his children on the beach. Or had the children said something?

He did not entertain this as a likely possibility. Children were children. They just followed their parents. He was sure they were happy they were going to be free from the restricted life they had been leading, free to watch television on a Friday night and Saturday, free to eat whatever they wished.

An idea suddenly struck him. He would invite these people in and put over to them how much of a non-Jew he was, without, of course, mentioning anything about the background.

Dorothy had walked to the shops and was not to be expected back for at least three-quarters of an hour. He would invite them in and have fun.

For the first time in days, the heaviness which had seemed to encompass his mind lifted a little, and he began to feel quite cheerful.

"Please come in," he said to the rabbi and Batsheva and Alex, who had come with him. "Can I offer you a cup of grape juice? It really is so hot."

"Don't worry," said the rabbi. "We just drank something at home." At the same time, he ushered the children into the apartment and sat opposite Richard.

"Do you live here?" Richard asked, knowing very well that a religious Jew couldn't possibly be anything but on holiday in this resort.

"No, I actually live in Weltham, about a hundred kilometers from here," the rabbi answered. "I am the principal of a school."

The children had gone together to Lucy and Steven's room, leaving the rabbi and Richard alone.

"Oh, that's very interesting," said Richard. "A convent?"

"It's a Jewish school," said the rabbi carefully.

"Oh, that's interesting," said Richard. "Where I come from there aren't really any Jews, so we don't know anything about them."

The rabbi nodded.

"I am very happy the children have found friends,"

Richard went on. "Would it be possible for you all to come and visit us? In fact, we would like to invite you out for a meal with us at the hotel restaurant. The food is excellent. They have a good selection of fresh lobsters and shellfish, delicious pork and the most mouth-watering leg of lamb. They usually put it in a cheese and wine sauce. For dessert, they serve the most exquisite ice cream, real *milchig* ice cream," he added, not really noticing what he had said.

"Not for supper, thanks," said the rabbi, trying not to smile. "But we would love to get together with you this evening, only it would have to be at our cottage. We have problems getting a baby sitter."

"That would be nice," said Richard. "We would like to reciprocate. Perhaps you would come on a picnic with us on Saturday afternoon."

"We'll find a day to do that," said the rabbi.

He got up, shook hands with Richard, called his two children and left.

"That shocked him," said Richard to himself as he walked back into the room.

He sat in his chair and looked towards the sea, feeling a certain uneasiness creeping up on him. What had he done? He had just committed himself to spending a whole evening with religious Jews. What would Dorothy say?

Though Dorothy, too, was shocked when she heard the news, she was at the same time rather pleased that they were to visit the Shulmans that evening. She kept exclaiming how she had really liked meeting Feige Shulman. On thinking it over, she was not surprised to find out that the Shulmans were religious Jews, even though they had somehow appeared in the middle of nowhere. She wondered if they would be like the Kesslers.

She had to admit, however, that she was somewhat

shaken. Unbeknown to anyone, she had reached something of a religious crisis on the previous night. She had gone to bed and tossed and turned for what seemed like hours. It was almost as it had been after the electric shock, where she had been filled with spiritual confusion as to who she was and what she believed.

Together with this was the very real pain she was experiencing over the possibility of eating *treif* and breaking *Shabbos*. She had felt herself becoming totally desperate, as if she was again on a train, but this time driving at full speed into a tunnel which was becoming blacker and blacker. She could not see where she was going, or what life held for her.

Eventually she prayed in a way she had not prayed before, with a sincerity which she had never felt before. "Hashem, if you want us as Jews, please take the initiative. Please show us what is right, and come and get us. I give up. I can't do any more."

Immediately after she had done this, she felt her spirits lighten. It was as if she had put her burden in the hands of Hashem.

When she woke up, she still felt a strange sense of peace. However, as the day wore on, she put it out of her mind. Surely it had been simply her imagination.

Now in the middle of nowhere, their children had found Jewish friends, *frum* Jewish friends. There had to be something in this.

It was strange how her longing for *Yiddishkeit* had deepened. She felt, somehow, that she really was Jewish and wanted to find out about it. She desperately wanted to find her parents or her family, but this had failed, and she knew now that she would never find them.

Beginning the conversion process had been inspiring but difficult, due mostly to the fact that she could no longer start keeping various *mitzvos* at her own pace but had to conform to the regimen as laid down by the *beis din*. Everything had begun to feel quite tedious, as a burden, and she had in some ways felt relieved when Richard had demanded that they give it up.

But as the days went on, it felt as if she was trying, slowly, to tear out her very heart. *Yiddishkeit* had become part of her. Without it, life felt completely empty.

She could no longer be satisfied with what she had before. Her husband and children were no longer enough. True, she didn't love them any less, in fact, in many ways, she loved them very much more, but she knew she had changed and she could not turn back.

She wondered if Richard could possibly be feeling the same way. She had never known him so angry, irritable, disillusioned and bitter. Nothing seemed to satisfy him. Could he also be missing *Yiddishkeit*?

Richard was having second thoughts about seeing the Shulmans that evening. He had wanted to shock the man, but nothing he had said had provoked the slightest reaction.

He somehow didn't feel like trying the same thing again. He wondered what he would say to Mr. Shulman, or was he Rabbi Shulman? Was a school principal a rabbi? Perhaps.

For one wild moment, he thought of discussing his position fully with him, letting him know the whole story. But he quickly put the idea out of his mind. He would just discuss general topics with him, talk about the weather, or politics, anything but religion. Surely Mr. Shulman would know about sports.

Sports? Why hadn't he been watching sports on television? Sports had been his life, and yet he was missing an important match. He had hardly given it a thought.

He went straight over to the television and put it on,

turning it onto the sports program. This was what life was really about, wasn't it?

He watched, trying to concentrate on the game. Concentrate on the game? He never in his life had to work to concentrate on the game. The game would enthrall him, take up his full attention. Now what was the score? Who was playing? Which side was winning?

He got up and walked to the window, watching the waves far out at sea. As if hypnotized, he stood watching for several minutes.

He was glad he had broken with *Yiddishkeit*, glad he was taking the family away from the terrible restrictions that being Jewish imposed on them. He had not informed the *beis din* of his intentions. They would just have to find out themselves. They just would not hear from them.

It would be wonderful to be able to eat anything he wanted, to be able to drive on *Shabbos*, to watch the sports programs. He was extremely, undeniably happy. Or, rather, even though he didn't really feel happy at the moment, he knew he had to be happy because he was free.

But why was he feeling so bitter and angry and unhappy? He was probably getting a cold, or a touch of flu. When he felt better, he felt sure, he would be happy.

He went back to sit in the chair in front of the television, but his mind kept on wandering, this time to the Shulman family.

It was a good thing they had no idea of their story, or of their position. He did not dream that at that very moment, Rabbi Shulman had just put down the phone after a long conversation with Rabbi Kessler.

CHAPTER 33

At eight o'clock in the evening, the Wilson family arrived at the Shulman cottage. Both Dorothy and Richard were reminded of their first visit to the Kesslers, a visit which seemed to have taken place years and years ago, although it was in reality less than a year ago.

Richard was quieter than usual. His anger and bitterness had left him, replaced by a black depression.

Dorothy felt her heart starting to beat fast. She was nervous. Why?

Steven and Lucy, on the other hand, were excited to spend the evening with their friends. Immediately after the door was opened, they were rushed inside to Batsheva and Alex's room.

Richard felt a little ashamed of the conversation he had had with the rabbi earlier in the day.

Surely the rabbi had excused this. How should Richard, a non-Jew, know any better?

He wondered what they would actually talk about. Would the subject of religion come up in the conversation? Surely the rabbi or his wife were bound to mention something about it.

Dorothy was half hoping they would, but they didn't.

The Wilsons were entertained in a warm and courteous manner. The rabbi and Feige conversed with them on many subjects, including sports, and Richard was actually surprised at their secular knowledge.

But the subject of religion or *Yiddishkeit* was not discussed. In fact, on at least three occasions, Richard tried to raise the subject, and on each of these three occasions, the rabbi would neatly turn the conversation in another direction.

Well, they were coming across as non-Jews. A Jew does not try to convert or influence a non-Jew in any way. So why should the Shulmans discuss religion with them?

Both Richard and Dorothy left with a certain sense of loss, of emptiness. They could have had so much to discuss, so much to share, so much to learn, but as gentiles, they could not do it.

They were both very silent when they returned home and spoke very little to one another that evening.

Dorothy woke up to find Richard standing beside her bed, offering her a cup of coffee. She looked at her watch. It was eight-thirty already! She was usually an early riser. Why had she overslept?

But she had fallen asleep very late last night. She had tossed and turned, trying to come to grips with her situation.

If only they could have spoken to Rabbi Shulman. But

ON A GOLDEN CHAIN

Richard would have been angry. There was no way that he would want to be Jewish again.

He had had enough. She would just have to accept her role again as a Presbyterian wife and mother and forget about the growing emptiness inside her very soul, an emptiness which had become like a persistent pain.

She took the cup of coffee gratefully.

"You're dressed already, Richard?" she said.

"Yes," said Richard. "The children are too. I wanted to take them to do a spot of fishing in the next village. Would you like to come too?"

"No, you know I don't like fishing," she said. "When are you going?"

"We are going right away," he said. "We have already had some cereal for an early breakfast. You were fast asleep, and I didn't want to bother you. You need a rest. I brought you a cup of coffee. Please carry on sleeping. We will be back just before lunch."

Within minutes they were gone. Dorothy lay back on the pillows and shut her eyes, but sleep would not come.

She began to think about the visit to the Shulmans the previous evening. He was a rabbi, he had told them that, even though he was a school principal. If only she had used the opportunity to speak to him. If only she could have told him everything.

He seemed to be the kind of person to whom one could tell everything. She suddenly sat bolt upright in bed. What was there to stop her? Why couldn't she speak to him?

Her family would not be back for at least three and a half hours. Richard would never, ever know. She was sure the Shulmans would not tell him if she asked them not to. A rabbi had to keep things confidential, surely.

But should she? What was she looking for? Didn't she

want to be a comfortable Presbyterian? The thought of this made her dress quickly, and within twenty minutes she was outside the apartment building, walking towards the Shulman's cottage.

Feige Shulman met her at the door. "Dorothy, please come in. It's so nice to see you. Where are Richard and the children?"

"They have gone fishing," said Dorothy. "They went early. I just wondered if I could talk to you both, confidentially, of course."

"Of course you can, come in," said Feige, putting on a kettle and taking some biscuits out of a tin. "Yisrael is still *davening*, that is, saying the morning prayers. He will be finished soon, and then we can all talk."

Dorothy drank some more coffee and ate some biscuits, aware that she had forgotten to eat breakfast. The Shulman children, disappointed that Steven and Lucy were not with her, had gone back to play in their rooms.

"Feige," said Dorothy, inwardly trembling. "Feige, maybe I will shock you with what I am going to say, but I think there is a possibility that I am Jewish."

Feige nodded, and waited.

Dorothy continued. "It's a long story," she said. "It's a very long story. Maybe I should wait until Rabbi Shulman finishes *davening* so I can tell you both."

"I don't think he will be long," said Feige.

At that moment the baby started to cry. Feige excused herself and went to her. "I must feed her," she said. "I won't be long. I'm sorry."

As Dorothy was left alone, she had an almost overwhelming desire to run away. She only now realized the extent of what she was doing in speaking to the rabbi. This was not to be some brief conversation and swapping of ideas. This was serious, very, very serious. On this lay a decision, to be or not to be a Jew.

Richard's antagonism was, of course, a big factor. But he *was* Jewish. His mother was Jewish. That couldn't really be changed.

She was feeling nervous and cold. She had a flashback to the feelings she had had as a child, waiting outside the school principal's office after not doing her homework three times in succession.

Why did she feel like this now? She could not help smiling. She *was* waiting outside the school principal's office, so to speak.

She was staring into her coffee cup and did not realize that the rabbi had come into the room and was watching her. He was wearing his *tallis* and *tefillin*, and she, like her children had been, felt herself profoundly moved by this.

"Please could I speak to you, rabbi?" she asked, noting that her voice had a tremor in it.

"Only with pleasure," said the rabbi, ushering her into the lounge. "Please come in."

She sat in an armchair, facing him, her anxiety mounting. Why *was* she so anxious?

She looked up at him. His eyes seemed to reflect worlds upon worlds. She started to speak, found she could not and started to cry and cry until she felt she would never stop, aware only that the rabbi had handed her a box of tissues and was waiting until she felt she could speak.

Slowly and steadily, her story came out, piece by piece. The rabbi and his wife, Feige, who had joined them, were both quiet, pretending to be hearing the story as if it was their first time.

After what, to her, seemed like an eternity, Dorothy got to the end of it. "I can't live without *Yiddishkeit*," she said. "I can't live without *Shabbos* and *kashrus* and I can't live without Hashem."

"You were beginning, you said, to find this all a tremendous burden," said the rabbi. "Everything extra you had to do just made things worse and worse."

"I don't feel like that now," said Dorothy. "It's like an example Rabbi Kessler gave to us about a man going up a steep hill with a large sack of stones on his back. When he sees another one that he has to pick up, he groans, picks it up reluctantly and puts it into the sack, moaning all the time about the extra weight. But if it is a sack of diamonds, every new stone causes him great delight, and he doesn't even feel the weight. In fact, the more it weighs, the happier he is."

"That's exactly it," said the rabbi.

"You know," said Dorothy. "Initially we were doing things we wanted to, changing things as they were convenient. But when we got in touch with the *beis din* and with my conversion, we *had* to do things. Everything became exactly like that, a succession of burdens, a whole lot of rules which seemed to be stifling all of us, especially Richard."

"How do you feel now?" asked the rabbi.

"I don't know," said Dorothy. "Well yes, I do know. At least I think I know. It's as if I've been up a mountain collecting stones. When I first started, I realized those things were important, that I was collecting semi-precious stones. Then I lost sight of that, it all seemed like worthless rocks, so I threw the bag down the hill. Then, after a while I looked back and saw that diamonds, rubies, sapphires and emeralds were rolling down the hill away from me, jewels that would have been mine. Now, I can never get them back."

"You can get all those back, and more," said the rabbi. "But I want you to think of something."

Dorothy nodded.

"You told me that Rabbi Kessler had talked about the commandments and the Commander who gave them," he said. "What was happening then, in your relationship to the Commander, when you were seeing all these things as burdens?"

Again Dorothy started to cry, and it took some minutes before she could control herself. "I don't know," she said at last. "I was just doing things I had to do. I wasn't even connecting them to Hashem. I mean, I knew it was the Torah, and of course, I believe in Hashem. I mean, in my head I believed in Hashem."

"Are you familiar with the terms *emunah* and *bitachon*?" asked the rabbi.

"That's belief and trust," said Dorothy. "Rabbi Kessler told us about that."

"I want you to work on *bitachon*," said the rabbi.

"How do I do that?" asked Dorothy. "I mean, I heard someone talk about the difference, or I read it somewhere. The person gave the example of a bridge. I could *believe* I could drive across the bridge and get to the other side and that the bridge would hold, but with *bitachon* I would actually drive my car over the bridge and get to the other side. It would sort of be like the theory and the practice."

"Think about that as much as you can. And at the same time, think about the first paragraph of the *Shema*. Remember, it is written in the singular, to you as an individual, and it tells you to love Hashem with everything you've got. Think about that, and you will start to see and appreciate the value of a *mitzvah*. It comes from Hashem. This is Hashem's will. By doing it, we attach, or bind ourselves, to Hashem. The commandment is the glue, as it were, that attaches the Commander to the commandee. That's you," he added.

"I'll think about that," said Dorothy, who was visibly

affected by what the rabbi was saying.

She got up to leave, paused and sat down again.

"What about Richard?" she asked. Her eyes suddenly widened. "What can I do that is new, something that I haven't really done before? Maybe I should *daven* a little. I don't really do that often. And I want to do something else, also."

"*Baruch Hashem*," said the rabbi quietly. "We will discuss it."

"But what about Richard?" said Dorothy. "Richard hates *Yiddishkeit*. He will never agree that we keep living as Jews. He will be so angry." She looked at Rabbi Shulman. "Please could you come and speak to him about this? Maybe you could make him see things differently."

"I could do that," said the rabbi. "But I think, in this instance, it is better to wait until he comes to see me."

"Why should he do that?" asked Dorothy.

"We'll give it a day or so," said the rabbi. "I have a feeling he will be over here talking to me, or even shouting at me, by tomorrow."

"You mean, to argue with you?" asked Dorothy.

"Probably," said the rabbi. "And I also want to ask your permission to tell him you spoke to me."

"Yes, of course," she said. "Are you sure he will come?"

"I think so," said the rabbi. "In the meantime, we will all be saying *tehillim*. *Tehillim* always has an amazing effect."

CHAPTER 34

"No, I am not deceived," said Richard, his voice angry and bitter. "Dorothy, I am not deceived. There is something happening here and I know it has something to do with the Shulmans."

It was almost ten p.m. on the evening of the same day.

"Dorothy," said Richard, his voice even louder. "I will go over to that rabbi and blast his religion apart. He has been trying to influence you and to influence the children. I thought a Jew never tried to influence a non-Jew! Don't think I didn't notice you were *davening*. Don't think I can't see that something is going on!"

Dorothy was silent. She didn't quite know what to answer.

Richard continued. "I can never, ever get away from this restrictive, fanatical, narrow-minded, chauvinistic religion. I am going to the rabbi, and I am going to tell him once and for all that I am a Presbyterian, that I am not a Jew and never will be a Jew. I will tell him that my wife and children will never again be trapped by a series of meaningless restrictions."

He was becoming more and more angry. Dorothy was relieved that the children were already asleep.

"I will not have rabbis ruling my life!" he shouted, bashing his fist into the side of the cupboard. He pulled back quickly, holding his hand in pain.

"Are you all right?" asked Dorothy. She had never seen Richard do that before.

"Yes, I am, of course I am," said Richard. "It was only that the cupboard was in the way and hurt my hand."

Dorothy resisted the temptation to point out that it was not the cupboard who had made the first move.

Richard put on his jacket, moving it somewhat gingerly over his reddened fist.

"Are you going out?" she asked. "Where are you going?"

"To the rabbi," said Richard. "Where do you think?"

"It's late."

"If he's anything like Kessler, he will be up learning for a few more hours," said Richard. "It isn't late for these rabbis. I will come back if the lights are out."

He stormed out of the room, closing the door with a definite but slightly cautious bang, being mindful of the other occupants of the apartment building. He had to fix that rabbi this minute. How could he interfere with his family?

He went out into the street and walked briskly towards the Shulman's cottage, debating with Rabbi Shulman in his mind, telling him about the archaic religion he represented.

He wanted to tell him that Judaism had nothing at all to do with him, nothing at all to do with the Wilson family.

ON A GOLDEN CHAIN

All kinds of thoughts and arguments came crowding into his mind. Perhaps he should just take his family and leave, leave for some other place along the coast, a place which would be free of Jews and rabbis.

But perhaps, along the coast there would be another Jew, even another rabbi.

He reached the cottage. The lights were still on in several rooms. Feeling anger surge up inside him, he knocked at the door.

Rabbi Shulman opened it and invited Richard inside, not looking the remotest bit surprised to see him at this hour and apparently not reacting to his anger. They were both soon seated. The rabbi waited for Richard to speak.

"Rabbi Shulman, you might have realized this is not our first encounter with Judaism and Jewish people."

The rabbi looked at him, and for a moment, Richard felt something stirring in his soul, something which he had felt sure he had managed to kill. He avoided Rabbi Shulman's eyes, finding a point somewhere by the window to which he could address himself.

"I hate Jews," he declared. "Not you, of course rabbi, not your family, but in general, I hate Jews. I hate Judaism. I hate *Yiddishkeit*, I hate *kashrus*, *Shabbos*, and each and every other restrictive law."

"But as a non-Jew you don't have to keep these," said the rabbi. "You say you are a Presbyterian. You don't have to keep *kashrus* or *Shabbos*. In fact, a gentile is not allowed to keep *Shabbos*."

"That's not fair," said Richard. "You are against gentiles."

The rabbi did not pursue the argument. Richard went on and on about how terrible Jews and Judaism were. Rabbi Shulman listened.

"Listen, rabbi," continued Richard. "We do not have the

same G-d. G-d is infinite. So infinite that we can never be close to Him."

"He is so infinite we can never be anything but close to Him. He is everywhere," said the rabbi. "Even if we don't feel it."

"Hashem isn't close to me," said Richard suddenly. "I tried to be close to Hashem, I tried everything. We were keeping *kashrus* and *Shabbos*. I was putting on *tefillin* every day, and I had started really learning."

"Did you enjoy that?" asked the rabbi, not pointing out that this was odd behavior for a gentile.

"Yes," said Richard. "When I was living, or beginning to live, as a *frum* Jew, I was happier than I had ever been." Again he looked at the rabbi but turned quickly away from his gaze. "But I wasn't completely *frum*. I mean, sometimes, in the beginning, I used to watch a football game on *Shabbos* afternoon. No one knew about it, not even Dorothy. And I was afraid to show my *Yiddishkeit* too openly. There were times I went without my *yarmulka*. I didn't want to give up everything for *Yiddishkeit* and be labelled."

The rabbi caught and held Richard's gaze.

"You are a Jew?" he asked, feeling it was important at this point for Richard to answer that question.

"I am, sort of," said Richard, hesitantly. "People, I mean, the rabbis and the *beis din* say that I am, and I know that my mother was a Jew. But she converted. She gave it all up and married a gentile, and we were gentiles. I don't know if I feel like a Jew. I mean, sometimes I do and sometimes I don't. Sometimes I even feel I am playing a game, that it isn't real. I mean, I don't belong in *Yiddishkeit* and my wife and my family don't really belong. They do and yet they don't. I don't want to be a Jew, but I am a Jew, but on the other hand I am not a Jew. I was brought up as a Presbyterian. Our minister didn't see me as a Jew. He saw me as a Presbyterian."

"Did you ever discuss this with your parents?" asked the rabbi.

"Not really," said Richard. "It was the kind of thing you didn't talk about. It was something of a skeleton in the closet. My mother had told me she was a Jew, and she told me how most of her family had been wiped out during the Second World War. She had also given up a lot of Jewish practices. When she met my father, of course, she gave up everything and became a Presbyterian. But I have her papers. She is Jewish, definitely. Where we were living, you just didn't speak about it. It wasn't quite proper to be Jewish, if you know what I mean."

"Richard," said the rabbi. "Do you have a Hebrew name?"

"Reuven," said Richard quickly.

"Reuven," repeated the rabbi. "I am just repeating what all the rabbis say. You are Jewish. You do belong and you belong completely."

"I don't feel it," said Richard. "At least, sometimes I might, but it isn't real."

His expression suddenly changed.

"I don't want to," he shouted. "I don't want all of this. I know that you rabbis can sweet-talk people into feeling they would do anything for *Yiddishkeit*, would change their whole lives and way of living, but it's just sweet-talk. It isn't real."

"What if it is?" asked the rabbi.

"What if it isn't?" said Richard.

Rabbi Shulman smiled. They were beginning to sound like some of his young pupils.

"Let's start all over again," he said. "Perhaps you could tell me about your contact with Judaism. We have a lot of time, haven't we? We are on holiday. How about starting from the beginning?"

Richard began, telling the rabbi again about his mother once having been Jewish, about his school days and the boys in the class finding out, about his meeting Dorothy, his marriage, his children, and the strange dreams Dorothy was having about trains.

Though this was the third time, or even the fourth including Rabbi Kessler, that Rabbi Shulman had heard the story, he listened intently, marvelling at the way he could hear a story four times in four different ways.

When he came to the recent events, about Steven being beaten up, Richard started to stumble over his words. His face became bright red, not with anger, this time, but in deep hurt over the way his child had been attacked.

"You see," he said to the rabbi. "You see, we can't be Jewish any more. I can't let my children suffer."

"You are Jewish, you can't change that," said the rabbi. "And it is highly likely that your wife and children are Jewish."

There was silence. "It would help if I knew for *sure* she was Jewish," he said. "Then we would belong *somewhere*."

"Would you like to be Presbyterian?" the rabbi asked.

"Of course not," said Richard.

"Can you believe there is someone else, besides Hashem? Can you worship someone else besides Hashem?"

"It's not like that," he said. "It's just that I can't be Jewish and my family can't be Jewish. I have saved them from a ghastly future. I know they are all relieved."

Rabbi Shulman, for the first time, told him about the visits he had had, first from Richard's children then from his wife.

Richard was amazed. "You mean, Steven would prefer to be beaten up as a Jew than to give it all up?"

"There is no doubt about that," said the rabbi.

"My son has more courage than I have," said Richard.

They spoke for a long time, discussing Richard's whole

attitude to Judaism, the fact that he had seen it as something he had added onto himself rather than his very essence. He found he had become involved with various aspects of Jewish life, at times very reluctantly, without giving thought to his connection with Hashem.

As they spoke, Richard felt more and more concerned about the way he had behaved over the past few days, culminating in his watching the soccer game on television on *Shabbos* afternoon. He was beginning to see things in perspective and becoming aware of the horror to which he was subjecting his family in tearing them away from *Yiddishkeit*.

Somewhere in the wee hours of the morning he turned to Rabbi Shulman. "Rabbi," he said. "I didn't realize what I was doing. I was just trying to fight back, to rebel in every way. I want to tell you I am sorry."

"It isn't me to whom you owe an apology," said the rabbi.

CHAPTER 35

As soon as Richard walked into the apartment at around four a.m., Dorothy, who had fallen asleep in an armchair waiting for him, noticed a change in him.

Not only did he seem calmer, but he had about him a certain sense of relief.

"You spoke to the rabbi," she said.

"Yes," he said. "And he told me only afterwards that you had also spoken to him, and so had the children."

"The children?" said Dorothy mystified. "They spoke to him on their own?"

"Apparently," said Richard. "They also could not tolerate the thought of being separated from Hashem and from *Yiddishkeit*."

"The children!" repeated Dorothy. "What about Steven being beaten up?"

"Steven told him very sincerely—and as a school principal, he knows when a child is sincere—that he would rather be beaten over and over than to be cut off from *Shabbos, kashrus* and everything else."

"Then we have no option," said Dorothy. "We have to go back to the *beis din*. In a few months time, I will be completely Jewish."

"Wait," said Richard. "We will do that, I am sure, but we haven't finished discussing things. The rabbi says we must take a few days and discuss things fully. Rabbi Shulman suggests we don't go back until my leave is finished. He has all kinds of plans, and he feels we must make one more effort to find your family."

"We've tried everything," said Dorothy. "We've tried absolutely everything. There is no lead, no lead at all. We have exhausted everything."

"We didn't have time to discuss everything in detail, but Rabbi Shulman wants us to do that. He wants us to give him every single detail of what you experienced, every single detail of what happened. We'll organize that as well."

Over the next few days, she could see that Richard's long talk with the rabbi had helped him become a much happier and more settled person. He was beginning to accept his Judaism with more enthusiasm. At one point, Richard expressed his feelings to her.

"I am sorry, Dorothy," he said. "I am sorry I was trying to drag you all away from Judaism. I thought I was doing the best for you. But you know, what I am beginning to feel now about *Yiddishkeit*, I have never, ever felt before. I am beginning to see that Torah and *Yiddishkeit* is life itself."

He looked at her, and she saw that he had truly changed. She had never seen in him before that kind of true inner radiance.

"Whether you convert or you find your family," he said, "we are going to make a lot of changes. I have been thinking a great deal about them. I want the children to go to the same school as the Kessler children. I would like us to move into Stamford Hill, into the Kessler's area. I will wear a *yarmulka* everywhere. My son was so brave to wear it to a secular school. I would like us to do absolutely everything. I want you to put on a *sheitel*. Rabbi Shulman told me that because Torah is connected to the Infinite, there is always room for improvement. So even when we have been *frum* for years and years, we will always be doing more and more."

His eyes were shining as he said this, and Dorothy smiled. Could her husband have actually fallen in love with *Yiddishkeit*? She felt overwhelmingly happy.

She awoke fairly late the next morning to find Lucy and Steven standing over her.

"Oh, at last you are awake," said Lucy. "Daddy has gone over to the Shulmans. He told us to wait for you and to give you your breakfast."

"Then we have a family conference," said Steven importantly.

"A family conference?" asked Dorothy. "What do you mean?"

"A Shulman–Wilson family conference," said Lucy. "A detective conference."

"To find your family," said Steven.

"How are you going to do that?" asked Dorothy, puzzled. Surely no one seriously considered it possible.

"Rabbi Shulman says that we must discuss it and discuss it until we have all the pieces like a jigsaw puzzle, and then we would all start putting it together. You should come now."

Some forty minutes later they arrived at the Shulman cottage to find Richard sitting opposite the rabbi, learning.

Dorothy pinched herself to see if she was really awake.

Feige smiled at her.

"It didn't take too long, did it?" she asked.

"Not at all," said Dorothy, unable to blot out from her mind the picture she had just seen.

"Feige," she said. "There are many, many questions I would like to ask you about *Yiddishkeit*, all sorts of questions. Most of them are little things that before seemed insignificant. Now I see that they are very important."

The two women spoke until lunchtime, when everyone converged on the kitchen to eat together. Afterwards, they settled down to the conference.

Rabbi Shulman asked both Richard and Dorothy to tell the story again, this time filling in every detail they could. Even the children had something to add. Eventually, the story seemed to be finished. They had tried their best to repeat every single incident, every conversation, every dream and even every thought that Dorothy had had that they could remember.

The rabbi was silent for several minutes. "There are some things I want to hear about again," he said, at last. "If they tie together as I think they might, we might have one more avenue to explore."

Dorothy looked at him sharply. They had been over the circumstances hundreds of times in their minds. Was there something else?

"Tell me again," he said, "about your dream, the part where you are looking into your own face."

"Well," she said, "I would be at the train station, after the crash, and I would be looking at all the people lying there, and one of the people, one of the faces would be my face, only it would be covered in blood." She shuddered.

"There's something, also, that Richard mentioned, something you said while you were rambling on and on while you were in hospital after the shock," he said. "You interpreted it as her confusion between her Hebrew and her English name, her conflict between her old life and the new. Didn't she said something about 'I am Dorothy'?"

"Oh, yes," said Richard. "That was one of the things she said very clearly. 'I am Esther and you are Dorothy, but we look exactly alike, so who is who, and who am I?'"

"And you said you had another dream that persisted," the rabbi said.

"Oh, yes," said Dorothy. "I forgot about that. Rabbi Kessler asked me also and I told him. It is probably not relevant. It was like 'Alice through the looking glass.' I would be a child, and I would be standing in front of a mirror, looking at my reflection. But then, as things happen in a dream, the reflection of myself would step straight out of the mirror. I would look into the mirror again and there would be two of us, and we would run to the window and look out. I still have that dream sometimes."

"I think we are getting there," said the rabbi. "Perhaps you haven't got such confusion of identity as you imagine. I want to go back now to old Kerry and her strange mumblings. What did you say she kept on saying?"

"Something, something like, 'We must be fair, one for one, and one for one.'"

Rabbi Shulman was silent. "And she said, that gave her comfort?" he asked.

"Yes," said Richard.

"You had one and she had one," the rabbi repeated. "Your parents had a little girl, but your mother still had an identical little girl. She might have seen the little girl with her when they were looking for you. It gave her a little comfort in that the whole 'crime,' as it were, did not seem so bad." He paused. "Do you think you could have had a twin, an identical twin?"

Dorothy felt as if time had suddenly stood still. It wasn't that all these incidences seemed to add up, it was far more than that, far deeper than that, but she could not reach far enough into her mind to pull out what was somehow tugging at her memory.

"Perhaps," she said at last.

The rabbi had been watching her carefully. There had been something in her expression, something which had given a hint of a glimmer of light somewhere far, far back in the distant past. It was not a question, it was a memory.

"Maybe we should look at that," he said quietly.

"I can't remember, oh, I can't remember," said Dorothy. "Oh, why can't I remember?"

"What would we do if there was a twin?" asked Richard. "We would have to advertise Dorothy's picture in the papers and see if there was anyone who looked exactly like her."

"We could do that," said the rabbi. "We could send it to the Jewish newspapers. That's a very good idea. But I would first like to make discreet inquiries among the rabbis of the various *shuls*, perhaps even in the South African *shuls*, because we are now looking for a carbon copy of Dorothy. Twins remain identical, basically, no matter where they have been brought up. I mean, it could be that out of the blue someone recognizes you or mistakes you for someone else."

Dorothy was becoming excited. There was a chance she might find her family. "But what if I didn't have a twin?" she asked. "What if it was just a conflict about my own identity?"

She turned to Richard but saw that his thoughts were far away. The rabbi signalled her not to interrupt him. After almost a minute, he came out of his reverie.

"Do you remember when we were in Safed?" he asked.

"Did you notice the way that cafe owner looked at you? You probably didn't see it, but I did. He looked at you in such a puzzled way, almost as if he was asking himself if he knew you. And do you remember the children? The little boy . . . he called you . . ."

"Morah Miriam?" asked Dorothy.

The rabbi was quick to grasp the situation. "You are talking about a city of mysteries," he said. "Tell me about it."

They told him.

"If that is so, that is amazing," he said. "But then, if you had a twin, of course you could be mistaken for her-Miriam, Esther, Esther, Miriam-sounds good. You have to go back to Safed."

"Go there?" said Richard. "I can't take leave forever! I have to go to work sometime. It was difficult enough to get down here."

"How much leave do you have left?" asked the rabbi.

"We have just under two weeks," said Richard.

"So you have just under two weeks to go," he said. "You have about ten days in Israel."

Richard stared at him. "You mean . . . ?"

"Yes," said the rabbi. "You won't get a booking on a plane, but I suggest you go on standby. I know a travel agent who could organize things for us. His children are in my school. I'll tell him to make it a top priority. The El Al connection leaves tomorrow night, I think. And then you can come back here and collect your car and your belongings and, of course, Steven and Lucy."

"We can't do that," said Richard. "It's too quick."

"When else do you want to do it?" asked the rabbi.

"Could you phone your travel agent friend and see how feasible it is?" asked Dorothy.

"Right away," said the rabbi as he left the room.

"It's too quick," Richard kept repeating.

Feige laughed. "My husband is always like that," she said. "People think he is impulsive, but we have all come to know that what looks impulsive has behind it a great deal of thought. We must work out what we can pack for you."

Richard sighed. Didn't anyone see that it was too quick?

The rabbi came back into the room, a broad smile on his face.

"Even better than I thought," he said. "He has just had two cancellations, a husband and wife whose baby has tonsillitis and an ear infection and is not allowed to travel for another week. They were due to catch the plane from my city tomorrow afternoon, to connect with the El Al flight arriving in Lod Airport early the following morning. I will drive you into the city immediately, and you can arrange the finances with your bank. I think you should release as much money as you can. You never know what you might need. You can always reverse it again. We will organize some things for you. The rabbi looked directly at Dorothy. "My wife has a *sheitel* similar to your hair. I think you should try it on. You'll have to wear one when you convert, but anyway, it is more than likely you are Jewish and should wear it now. Feige will find it for you. One more thing. From now on, you are Reuven and Esther."

CHAPTER 36

*T*he El Al plane circled Tel Aviv and landed at Lod Airport. Though everything had been arranged in such a hurry, they had had time on the journey to think and relax, and to speak about many things.

Both Reuven and Esther realized that they had both had a complete change of attitude about *Yiddishkeit*. They had made a real commitment. Despite the fact that Reuven had a lot of questions, to them everything had become alive and real.

They had both spent much of their time saying *Tehillim* from tiny English-Hebrew books that the Shulmans had given them. Their lives had been so profoundly affected by the Shulmans. They could not believe they had met them scarcely a week ago. Reuven and Esther wondered how the children were, but they were sure they were enjoying themselves.

Before they left, Reuven had put through a call to Rabbi Kessler, who had been delighted by what he had heard. Lucy and Steven had told the Kessler children that they were going to be their neighbors and were coming to their school. There had been great excitement all around.

They were to be met at the airport by Rabbi Yossy Hertz, a close friend of the Shulmans, who lived in Bnei Brak. Bnei Brak was going to be their base for their short stay in Israel.

Rabbi Hertz had been told the whole story by the Shulmans. He arranged the hiring of a car to make travel faster and more convenient. They certainly did not have time to spare.

They were to leave for Safed with the rabbi as soon as they had rested and eaten a little. They recognized Rabbi Hertz and two of his daughters the moment they got off the plane. They had been told by Rabbi Shulman to look for someone with red hair and a red beard, similar to his own. Even his daughters Sara and Chanie had flaming red hair.

Almost as if in a dream, they followed him to the car. They were soon being made to feel at home by his charming wife Raizel. Esther longed to go to sleep, but she and everyone else realized the urgency of the business at hand.

They were soon driving a little too swiftly along the northern coastal roads of Israel. They chatted with the rabbi, feeling very much at ease with him, relieved that he spoke both Hebrew and English fluently. Though he seemed to know their story very well, he insisted that they tell it to him over again in all its detail.

After nearly two hours of fast driving, the hills of Safed came into view. Eventually, they saw the old cemetery with the holy sites marked in blue.

"We'll go to the cafe owner who seemed to recognize

ON A GOLDEN CHAIN

you," said Rabbi Hertz. "I know him quite well. I will tell him a little of the story, and then bring you inside."

They waited in the car, Esther becoming more and more nervous. Was this a wild goose chase?

She saw Yossy Hertz signalling to her to come in. Very self-consciously, she got out of the car and walked into the cafe. The man looked at her and his face broke into a smile. "Almost identical, I would say. Actually, I've seen you before, maybe a few months ago. Even then I was struck by the similarity. You're a duplicate of Rebbetzin Miriam, Rabbi Trilby's wife. Menachem Trilby, that is. His brother is in Yerushalayim."

"Where can I find her?" asked Esther. "Do you know if she had a twin?"

"I don't know much about her," said the man. "All I know is that she is an outstanding teacher. All the kids in the area just love her. I'll give you the address. You can sort it out with her."

He started to write and stopped when a young woman wearing a *tichel* walked in.

"Oh, Chaya," he said. "This lady wants to get in touch with Miriam. Please could you show her where she lives?"

"A relative," said Chaya, looking at Esther, this being a statement rather than a question. "But didn't you hear?"

She whispered something to the man. He in turn whispered to Yossy Hertz. Yossy turned to Esther and Reuven.

"Miriam's father became very ill last night, extremely ill," he said. "She left this morning to be with him."

"Where are they?" asked Esther. "Which hospital?"

"Shaarei Tzedek Hospital in Yerushalayim," said Chaya.

They looked at Rabbi Hertz. "I have some things to do in Yerushalayim," he said. "In fact, I have a lot of things. I will drop you off at the hospital and pick you up there later."

"I think you had better eat here first," said the man. "I will fix you something very quickly." He went to the back of the shop.

Ten minutes later, they were on the road again, descending away from Safed, ready for the long ride to Yerushalayim.

Esther suddenly gasped. "Whom are we looking for at the hospital?" she asked. "I mean, I know it could be my father, but what is his name?"

"Rabbi Landsky, Rabbi David Landsky," said Rabbi Hertz. "I asked about that."

Esther was quiet during the long drive. She was busy with her thoughts. Could it be? Could it really be that she was on her way to see her father?

Perhaps it would be a mistake. Perhaps this wasn't her sister. Perhaps she would be a woman who looked a little like her, and when she approached her about having a twin, the woman would look at her in amazement and shake her head. What would she do if that happened? She would leave the hospital, leave Yerushalayim and leave Israel, that very day. She would go back to Carroll Beach.

She stopped. What kind of mind trip was she going on? But her mind continued. She would arrive at the hospital and see a family, her family, standing around looking totally devastated, because Rabbi Landsky was dying. Perhaps he had died already. She felt tears coming into her eyes. Surely Hashem wouldn't do that to her. Surely she would not find her father, only to find he had just passed away.

Another thought came to torment her. She would arrive just before Rabbi Landsky died. She would arrive in time to tell him that she was his long lost twin daughter, and he would pass away with a smile on his lips because his prayers had been answered.

She tried and tried to force this picture out of her mind,

ON A GOLDEN CHAIN

but it kept coming back. Was she to find him, only to lose him again right away?

What should she do? Perhaps she should say *Tehillim*, but the extent of her knowledge of *Tehillim* in Hebrew was *kapitl aleph*. She started to say this softly, over and over again.

CHAPTER 37

As Esther reached the doors of the hospital, she was suddenly seized with an attack of nervousness. She did not want to go in. She could not bear another disappointment such as Southbroom. She wanted to walk away with hope still in her heart that she might find her family.

And her father, if this was her father, was apparently desperately ill. Perhaps she would be too late.

She turned back to the parking lot where Reuven was waiting, where Rabbi Hertz had left them. She would leave Yerushalayim, leave Israel. They would visit the Greek Islands, anywhere to get away. Then she would return home and convert and start anew. A convert has no family, no parental family, that is. She, at least, had Reuven and the children. It would be as if she had been born into the world with a new *neshamah*.

Once again, she turned back to the hospital doors. She had to pursue it just one more time. It was, she knew, a slim chance based on a series of chances, but this would be her last move in her search. If this didn't work out, she would give up.

Why was it so difficult to enter those hospital doors?

"Pull yourself together, Dorothy-Esther," she said to herself. "Steel yourself. If it doesn't work out, run out and leave. Leave tonight."

She went through the doors to the reception desk.

"Landsky family," she said to the woman, who, in reply, waved towards a young woman wearing a dark *sheitel* sitting in the adjoining waiting area.

"Landsky family?" she asked the woman.

"Yes," the woman said, obviously not at home with the English language, and trying to work out why Esther looked so familiar. "Yes. What can I do for you?"

"Are you Rebbetzin Trilby?" asked Esther, her heart sinking. She might have had the same coloring, but she didn't look a copy of herself.

"Yes," said the woman.

Had she understood? Esther was suddenly seized with a desire to run away, to leave and not pursue it. But she was here to say her piece and she had to do it, after which she could run.

"Did you have a sister who was lost in a train crash many years ago, who had a star on a golden chain?"

The woman stared at her uncomprehendingly. "What? No. Why?" she said.

At that point, Esther ran out, knowing her face was scarlet. Her heart was beating fast. As she went through the double doors, she realized that tears were streaming down her face.

She didn't know how she got to the parking lot, but before she knew it, she and Richard were walking quickly away from the hospital to catch the bus to the Wall. They were to meet Rabbi Hertz close to the hospital in two hours time. They would be back.

Because of the anxiety about Rabbi Landsky and the fact that everyone was busy saying *Tehillim*, it was at least two hours later that Chava Trilby, Miriam's sister-in-law, who lived in Yerushalayim, told Menachem Trilby, Miriam's husband, about the strange woman who had asked her if she had lost a sister in a train crash and had run out of the hospital before she could question her further. Chava had come over to the hospital to see how she could help her brother-in-law's family.

Chava had known that her younger sister-in-law had had a twin who had apparently died, but she had never been told of the circumstances. She was not prepared for her brother-in-law's reaction of shock and despair.

How could she have known that the family had been searching for Esther for so many years? And, in retrospect, the woman did look remarkably like Miriam.

Her brother-in-law started to make inquiries around the hospital, but no one knew who she was or where she had gone.

"Here she comes now," said the receptionist suddenly.

The younger rabbi turned around to come face to face with his wife, Esther's twin.

"This doesn't add up. There is a mistake somewhere," said Rabbi Hertz when he met them two hours later. He looked worried. He hoped that they hadn't delayed things too much.

"I see I shouldn't have left you," he said. "I suppose it is very difficult. Can we try just once more?"

"I'm not going," said Esther. "I can't. I want to leave. I'll convert. I'll have no family, except Richard and the children."

"Please stay here," he said. "I'm going in." He went straight towards the doors.

His experience was totally different, however, for standing next to reception, looking towards the doors, was a duplicate copy of Esther. A person so identical must be a twin. He knew this was Miriam. He knew it had to be Esther's twin. He decided on the direct approach.

"Rebbetzin Trilby?" he asked. "Rebbetzin Miriam Trilby?"

"That's right," she said.

"Have you a relative, a twin perhaps, called Esther?'

Miriam turned white as a sheet. Her husband had told her that someone just like herself had come into the hospital, talked about a twin and a train crash, and had run out again. The young woman had spoken to her sister-in-law, also a Mrs. Trilby, but she had known nothing of the story and therefore had missed the importance of it.

She nodded, not knowing what to say.

"Did you ever live in South Africa?" the rabbi asked.

"Yes," she said. "We lived there until I was eight. My father was a rabbi in the Cape. He was there for more than twelve years. Esther and I were born there."

Yossy felt his heart beating faster.

"There was a train crash," he said. "A train crash at a place called Dikbos."

"That's right," said Miriam. "That's where Esther vanished. We were told she was drowned. But my parents never believed it and then there was that strange woman in the forest-Carey-no, Kerry, or something. My parents thought she had kidnapped Esther, but we could never find her, and then we also thought perhaps she had drowned... But-where is she?"

"Come outside with me for a minute," said the rabbi.

"He's going to come out and say it was all a mistake," said Esther. "I know he is. I can't bear it. We must go away from here. I can't take it."

She looked up and saw Rabbi Hertz standing with a young woman on the steps. Looking at the young woman was like looking right into a mirror. This was beyond any doubt her twin!

Miriam spotted her at the same moment and they ran into one another's arms, crying for the years they had been separated.

"How is Rabbi Landsky? I mean, my father?" asked Esther, suddenly remembering why they were there.

Miriam again started crying. "Oh, Estie, Tatty is very, very sick. He needs very, very complicated heart surgery. They will do it, but they hold out very little hope."

"I must see him," said Esther. "I have to see him."

At that moment, Rabbi Menachem Trilby came up to them, looked into the face of the weeping girls and, his eyes filling with tears, smiled.

"Oy, now there are two of them!" he said. "The twins are back—duplicates!" He shook hands with Rabbi Hertz and then with Reuven.

"Menachem Trilby," he said. "Your brother-in-law, I think."

"Richard. I-I mean Reuven," said Richard. "I think you are right. Your brother-in-law."

"We must tell Mama," said Menachem. "We didn't say anything about Chava seeing you in case... in case you didn't come back."

"Where is Chava?" asked Esther. "I would like to speak to her, to explain."

"She's with the children," said her brother. "She will be back in about an hour or so."

"Shouldn't I just go and see Mama?" asked Esther.

"It might give her too much of a shock to see you again," said Menachem. "It will be the best and most beautiful shock anyone could ever experience, but still a shock. We should do it slowly."

Esther took off the golden star from around her neck.

"What about showing her this?" she asked.

"I have one exactly like it," said Miriam. "I have it right here." She too, took off a star on a golden chain from around her neck, an identical golden star.

Menachem held the two stars on his hand.

"I'll call her out and show these to her," he said, unable to take his eyes off the two shining Jewish stars. "It will be too much for Tatty's heart to see them. We will have to ask the doctors."

"Do you remember anything about your early childhood that I can tell her?" asked Menachem.

"I can hardly remember anything," said Esther. "It has all been dreams and fleeting thoughts. I still have to tell you all about it. There is so much to tell, and yet so little."

"All right," said Menachem, "I will take these to her."

"Wait," said Esther. "I am not sure if this is a dream or an illusion, or if it was ever real, but I can tell you something. I dreamed that shortly before the train crash, on a *Shabbos*, I was playing with my ball, and it went onto the *Shabbos* table. It smashed the beautiful crystal *Shabbos* decanter, and the wine went over everything. There was a terrible, terrible mess, and I was so sorry and so upset. The wine and the glass were everywhere. The whole table had to be reset, and we had to start all over again with saying *Kiddush*."

Menachem looked at her for a few seconds. "I am sure she will remember something like that. I will mention it."

It was nearly twelve minutes later that Menachem walked through the double doors with his mother-in-law. She had obviously been through a lot of strain with her husband's illness, and had shed many tears, but the news of her daughter's return seemed to her hardly believable.

She looked at Esther intently for a few seconds and then smiled a radiant smile, as she threw her arms around her.

"*Mein* Esther" she said between sobs. "*Mein shaine* Esther, you have come back to us."

She led her away to a private corner, and there mother and daughter spent time together. Who can describe the moments that they shared?

"Your father must see you, Esther," said her mother. "Your father has got to see you."

CHAPTER 38

H "He's been given his pre-med already so he will be a bit drowsy," the young anaesthetist remarked as he escorted Esther into the private ward where her father was waiting to be called for his operation. "But it will also help to keep him calm. I mean, this is quite a story I have been hearing. I would like to hear the rest of it."

After a brief but intensive discussion between family and physicians, it was decided that meeting Esther before the operation, although involving the risk of shock, would ultimately be for his good. He had suffered a great deal due to the loss of his daughter and had never ceased to say *Tehillim* for her and to feel anguish about her. The doctors felt it might give him the extra motivation to cope with the extensive surgery he was about to undergo.

ON A GOLDEN CHAIN

There was also the sobering fact that the operation might not be successful, and then there would, Heaven forbid, be no other chance for father and daughter to meet.

Rabbi Landsky lay in the hospital bed. He had already been dressed in the robes necessary for the operating theater. As the pre-med drug took over, he found himself unable to concentrate on his *sefer*. He put it down on the table beside him and settled back just to think and meditate. He knew he was going in for major surgery-very major surgery. The danger of the situation had been explained to him, and he was ready to meet everything that came his way.

Ready? There was one thing which tugged at him, which had tugged at his heart and mind for many, many years. There was one thing which he would have wished above everything else. That one thing was to see his daughter who had disappeared in the train crash in Dikbos.

They had searched and searched, but she was neither among the living nor among the dead, and all the dead had been identified. Something inside him told him that she was somewhere out there, somewhere still in the world. But where? And with whom? This was the ache that had grown in his heart over the years, and he had felt it recently as severe physical pain. Surely, the two were connected!

Once again, the old feelings of anguish engulfed him, dulled a little by the medication he had been given, but still almost unbearable.

If only he could see her, just once! He felt, then, that he could do anything, go through anything.

He dozed for a few moments and then opened his eyes, as someone walked into the room accompanied by the doctor. It was Miriam! But... something was different... he sensed that it was not Miriam.

He felt tears start down his cheeks, and he saw that the

woman, too, started to cry. Even the doctor brushed away a tear as he left, quietly shutting the door behind him.

He knew who this was! A person looking exactly like Miriam, but not Miriam. She could only be Miriam's identical twin.

"Esther?" he whispered.

"Tatty, oh, my Tatty," she said.

Tears flowed down both their faces.

"It's been a long time, Esther," he said. He looked at her searchingly. "You are wearing a *sheitel*, Esther. You are *frum*?"

"Yes, Tatty," she answered.

"*Baruch Hashem*," he whispered. "*Baruch Hashem*."

Many hours later, Rabbi Landsky lay in his private hospital ward. He was in a great deal of pain, but at the same time he was aware of a strange warmth, a sense of peace, as if a great crushing weight had been lifted off his shoulders. Why was that?

He started to remember. He had had a dream, a dream about his long lost daughter, Esther. She had come to him and spoken to him, a *frum* woman wearing a *sheitel*.

He hovered in the world between the conscious and the unconscious. He had a longing to see her again, a yearning. But it was a dream, wasn't it?

But it had been so real, so clear. He dozed off again, but was soon awake again, feeling the pain in his chest more sharply. He heard the familiar voice, familiar though he had only heard it once in many years, and he opened his eyes.

Both Miriam and Esther were standing next to his bed, watching him anxiously, each with a *Tehillim* in her hand.

He was obviously dreaming again, dreaming that his twin daughters, now grown up, were visiting him. He closed his eyes, a smile playing on his lips.

ON A GOLDEN CHAIN

As the hours and the days went by, he became accustomed to seeing his twin daughters standing together in the intensive care unit as if they had never been separated. And yet he still felt it was a kind of vision or dream.

One day, a young man came to visit him, a man called Reuven, obviously a religious young man, who explained that he was Esther's husband. The rabbi remembered vaguely that one of the people who appeared and disappeared while he was in and out of consciousness had explained the whole story to him. There were two children, weren't there? But that had been a dream, hadn't it? Could it have been real?

But this young man was real, and this young man claimed to be his son-in-law, the husband of his lost daughter.

"Reuven," he said in a voice so weak that Reuven had to lean forward to hear him. "Reuven, my daughter was lost for so many, many years and how did she find out she was Jewish? And how did she marry a *frum* young man like you?"

"It's a long story, a very, very long story," said Reuven.

The rabbi smiled. "Tell it to me, Reuven. Tell me everything. Don't leave anything out. I have heard a little of the story, but I don't know what I dreamed and what I really heard. I want to hear it from you."

A nurse came in to give him an injection and the rabbi spoke to her. "Please tell my family, tell everyone not to come in until I ask them to. I want to spend time with my son-in-law. We have a lot to discuss together."

"Rabbi," said the nurse. "You must not tire yourself."

"Is it all right if he does almost all the talking?" the rabbi asked.

"Well, I guess that's all right," said the nurse. "But," she said to Reuven, "If you see him getting tired, then . . ."

"Then I will let him sleep," said Reuven.

He turned to his father-in-law, feeling an incredibly close

connection with the man for whom he had been saying *Tehillim*. His father-in-law, a rabbi, his own father-in-law, grandfather of Steven and Lucy, his own family!

He started to tell the story, and the rabbi lay back on the pillows, the machines beside him registering that his heartbeat was good and his breathing regular. Reuven found himself watching his father-in-law's blood pressure, deciding that if it started to go up, he would leave.

But it remained steady as Reuven told the rabbi even the smallest details. It felt so different and so good to talk to his father-in-law. For the first time, he was talking to someone to whom he belonged, someone who belonged to him. Over the past few days, the experience of being part of a *frum* family had settled so many things for him. They were no longer an isolated family finding their way into *Yiddishkeit*.

As he spoke, however, he realized that Esther's father was becoming tired. He left him to rest, promising to come the next day.

He did that, and every day after that. It was as if his father-in-law wanted to make up to him everything he had missed as a Jew. Reuven had confided to him his deepest fears and doubts, fears and doubts which were fast being evaporated by the rabbi's answers.

The rabbi spent hours with his daughter, too, the daughter who had so miraculously returned to him, and his times with the Wilsons seemed to build up his strength in a way which amazed the doctors.

Two weeks after Reuven and Esther landed in Israel, Reuven and Menachem went to Lod Airport to meet Lucy and Steven.

Rabbi Shulman had found people from his community who were travelling to Israel, who were more than happy to take Lucy and Steven with them.

The children had been told about their grandfather, and the Shulmans had been saying *Tehillim* with them for him. They had been in telephone contact with the whole family, especially their Bubby, who was always saying how she longed to see them.

Now, at last, they were all to meet in person. The children were overwhelmed to find themselves an integral part of a *frum* family and *frum* world.

Shortly after they arrived, they were brought by Reuven and Esther to their Zaidie's bedside. The hospital intensive care unit had strict rules about children under twelve visiting, but in this instance, at the recommendation of three specialists, the children were brought in.

The rabbi's eyes shone as he saw them. He pulled out the small Jewish star which he kept close by.

"Just think," he said. "Hashem worked all these miracles. He brought you all back to us through a tiny star-a star on a golden chain."

About Bais Kaila

JUST A SHORT DRIVE SOUTH of New York City lies the Torah community of Lakewood, New Jersey. Far removed from the profligate influences of the city, the tree-lined streets of this serene and picturesque town reverberate with the sweet sounds of Torah, not the clamor and blare of urban congestion. In this beautiful setting, the students of Bais Kaila High School are taught Torah and the traditional values of our precious heritage. In this environment, they can truly grow into the kind of Bnos Yisroel that have always been the backbone of our people.

Bais Kaila High School was founded in 1977 by Rabbi Yisroel Schenkolewski and Rabbi Shmuel Mayer, both alumni of the world famous Lakewood Yeshiva, to serve Lakewood and the other Central Jersey communites. Over the years, the school has developed a singular blend of high caliber educational programs, both in Limudei Kodesh and secular studies, and careful attention to the individual needs of each girl. The staff is talented and experienced, and class sizes are limited to ensure warm and productive teacher-pupil relationships. At Bais Kaila, each girl is motivated and encouraged to reach her full potential, intellectually, spiritually, emotionally and socially, with particular emphasis on good *midos* and solid ethical and moral values.

The future of Bais Kaila High School is bright and full of promise. Over the past few years, our enrollment has grown very rapidly, so that we are continuously expanding our facilities. Furthermore, the already outstanding curriculum is constantly reviewed and innovative refinements added. Indeed, the philosophy of a Bais Kaila education and its implementation place the school among the foremost educational institutions of its kind.